The Cowboy and His Beauty

A Second Chance, Beauty and the Beast Romance

Kaci M. Rose

Copyright

Copyright © 2023, by Kaci M Rose, Five Little Roses Publishing. All Rights Reserved.

No part of this publication may be reproduced, distributed, or transmitted in any form or by any means, including photocopying, recording,

or other electronic or mechanical methods, or by any information storage and

retrieval system without the prior written permission of the publisher, except

in the case of very brief quotations embodied in critical reviews and certain

other noncommercial uses permitted by copyright law.

Publisher's Note: This is a work of fiction. Names, characters, places, and incidents are a product of the author's imagination.

Locales and public names are sometimes used for atmospheric

purposes. Any

resemblance to actual people, living or dead, or to businesses, companies,

events, institutions, or locales is completely coincidental.

Book Cover By: **Sarah Kil Creative Studio**

Editing By: Debbe @ **On The Page, Author and PA Services**

Blurb

She is the girl who got away. He seems all too familiar. Could the man behind the beast be her cowboy in disguise?

Sky

I'm back in town licking my wounds after losing my job in Dallas. Only I haven't told my parents yet. They think I'm in town just visiting.

When I run into the man everyone calls The Beast; I can't shake the feeling that I know him from somewhere, even if his long hair, beard, and scar make it impossible to figure out where.

It's only proper Walker Lake ranching tradition to say hello to your neighbors, so I offer to cook him dinner. I never thought I'd get a job offer out of the deal.

And I never would have guessed the true identity of this growly beast.

Dash

I find it amusing that Sky doesn't recognize me, but I guess that's the whole point.

After my military time, I came home to take over the family ranch.

With Sky gone in Dallas, the ranch was my sole focus until I ran into her again.

With her around, I feel human once more, and I want people to see me.

When she finally figures out who I am, will she still want me?

Dedication

To Liz and Marissa,

You two have gotten me through life's ups and downs, so I dedicate this series to you.

I hope you find some laughter, a few characters like you, and a little revenge for some unfinished business.

Thank you for being my friends, even though we are states apart.

Contents

Get Free Books! — XI

1. Chapter 1 — 1
2. Chapter 2 — 9
3. Chapter 3 — 15
4. Chapter 4 — 25
5. Chapter 5 — 33
6. Chapter 6 — 43
7. Chapter 7 — 49
8. Chapter 8 — 57
9. Chapter 9 — 67
10. Chapter 10 — 73
11. Chapter 11 — 79
12. Chapter 12 — 87
13. Chapter 13 — 95
14. Chapter 14 — 105
15. Chapter 15 — 111

16.	Chapter 16	121
17.	Chapter 17	125
18.	Chapter 18	131
19.	Chapter 19	137
20.	Chapter 20	143
21.	Chapter 21	149
22.	Chapter 22	153
23.	Chapter 23	161
24.	Epilogue	167
	More Books by Kaci M. Rose	171
	Connect with Kaci M. Rose	174
	About Kaci M Rose	176
	Please Leave a Review!	179

Get Free Books!

Would you like some free cowboy books?

If you join Kaci M. Rose's Newsletter you get books and bonus epilogues free!

Join Kaci M. Rose's newsletter and get your free books!

https://www.kacirose.com/KMR-Newsletter

Now on to the story!

Chapter 1

SKY

Welcome to Walker Lake, Texas!

Country, Cowboys, and Community.

Established In 1882

The sign coming into town looks the same as when I was a kid, but the original was replaced following a storm when I was in high school.

It's comforting to know nothing has changed because *everything* has changed in the world outside of my small Texas hometown.

But I can't think about that right now. I have to be the perfect peppy daughter coming home for some vacation time to see her parents, not to tell them she failed at being an adult.

Walker Lake is different from most Texas farm towns. The lake separates two distinct classes of people—the cowboys on the outskirts of town with big ranches and the wealthy people with fancy lake houses who move here for the small-town charm only an hour outside Amarillo.

My parents own a lake house, but my best friends are on the cowboy side of town. Even my high school boyfriend's family were ranch owners and more down-to-earth than my parents.

That's why I haven't told them I quit my job. They won't care that the startup I worked for kept cutting my pay but expecting full-time hours. They won't care that the company was going under, and I got out while I could. They'll only care how it looks that their daughter left a job with the big-time tech guy they love to brag about. Because all they care about is appearances.

That's the life I grew up in, but it's not the life I want. I want a much simpler way of life, like my friends who grew up on the ranches outside of town. Getting there is the hard part.

The comfort of home is sadly lacking as I pull up in my parents' driveway. Yes, this is the house I grew up in, but it never felt like home. I grab my purse and suitcase before checking to ensure I didn't leave anything in my car when I loaded the stuff I was keeping from my Dallas apartment into the storage unit a few towns over. I figure it's close enough to get to if needed, but far enough away that word shouldn't get around town.

"I'm home!" I call as I walk through the front door. I know they're home, and they know I'm here. Seems they can't be bothered to greet me.

I set my suitcase on the floor by the stairs and head for the large family room in the back of the house overlooking the lake where my parents spend most of their time.

"Hello, darling. We expected you a few hours ago," my mom says without looking up from her tablet.

"I told you I'd be here closer to dinner. I had a few things to take care of before I could get on the road," I tell her as I lean in to kiss my dad on the cheek.

He gives me one of his soft smiles before returning to whatever he was doing on his phone.

I offer my mom a hug, but her eyes never leave the tablet in her hands. I sigh. What was I expecting?

I turn to stare out the large floor-to-ceiling windows overlooking the lake and try to release all the stress. I can't tell my parents what's going on yet. They think I'm here on vacation for a week.

I'm hoping to figure things out this week. If not, I can return to Dallas and stay with my best friend and her husband for a bit. Sarah and Mac have so much space; they said I could stay for months if needed. Not that I would. I need a new job before my parents figure out I'm jobless *and* homeless.

I've never been more thankful that I'm good with money and saved a several-month emergency fund while working. With no rent now, it will last even longer.

"Did you hear me, Sky?" my mom asks.

I turn to see she's finally set her tablet down and is staring at me. "No, sorry. I was lost in the view. It's always been relaxing."

"I asked if you could swing by the store and pick up a few things for dinner. There is a list on the counter. Maria won't be back for a few days."

"It's Martha, Mom. The girl who cooks for you guys is Martha," I remind her.

Mom waves her hand like it doesn't matter. Martha has been with my parents for almost ten years, and my mom never gets her name right. It seems my parents decided what they wanted for dinner and that I'll be cooking it since my mom never learned. Thankfully, Martha taught me, so I could fend for myself when I moved out.

They'd go out to eat in Amarillo if I weren't here. My parents aren't diner people, so eating in Walker Lake wouldn't work for them.

"Yeah, I can do that. Let me take my bag upstairs and get unpacked."

"Sounds good, dear," Mom says, already engrossed in her tablet again.

I take my bag upstairs to my room. I packed up all my stuff and took it with me, but the decor is still the same. The beautiful blue-gray on the walls took me weeks to choose, and the gorgeous blue sheets with purple and pink flowers I fell in love with are on the bed.

The furniture is familiar, but the posters I had on my wall growing up are now replaced with art my mom has bought over the years.

I quickly unpack and put my suitcase in the closet before texting Sarah to let her know I had arrived safely. Then I go downstairs, grab the list from the counter, and head out.

I pause for a moment and stare next door. Mac's family owns the lake house next to my parents. They don't live there permanently and only use it for vacations. Sarah spent a lot of time at my house growing up, and during the summers, we swam in the lake. Mac and Sarah met one summer when his family was there. They had an instant connection, though they were friends for many years before either acted on it. Spending time with them doesn't seem half bad the more I think about it.

Walker Lake is a typical small town. One grocery store and a main street—only our main street is more of a town square leading to the lake and is the heart of the town.

Then there's the rumor mill that comes with a small town. One visit to the store and everyone will know I'm home before the end of the day.

The grocery store hasn't changed much. The post office is still attached, so you can get all your groceries, bait, and tackle, and send your mail all in one place—live bait, at that. You can't get anything too fancy, but they place bulk orders for the cowboys who stock up and don't have time to head into Amarillo for supplies.

I head up and down the aisles, lost in thought. The layout hasn't changed since I was in school, so I know exactly where everything is. Thankfully, my mom doesn't want anything too extravagant tonight. She settled on chicken parmesan and garlic bread.

Easy enough, but the list also says to grab any breakfasts or snacks I want, so I do that as well. I'm trying to make a game plan for sending in resumes while staying with my parents when I turn and bump into a cowboy.

"I'm sorry," I say as I grab his arm to steady myself. I look up, expecting to know who I ran into, but while there's an air of familiarity, I have no idea who this man is.

His hair is long, and his beard conceals his face. His eyes are hard to see under his cowboy hat, and when he turns his head, the scar down the side of his face is hard to miss. I'm sure without all the facial hair it would be jarring. I guess that's why he grew out the thick beard.

I take a step back and trip over my feet. The cowboy reaches out to steady me with his hands on my arms, ensuring I'm stable before he lets go. Sparks erupt on my skin where he's touching me—sparks I haven't felt since my high school boyfriend, Corey.

I wrote those sparks off as teenage hormones and the flush of first love. I never thought I'd feel them again. Did this mysterious cowboy feel them, too, or was it a figment of my imagination?

He releases me suddenly, but his hands hover over my arms as if he's ready to catch me again should the need arise.

"Thank you. I'm sorry; I'm not usually this clumsy. I've been driving all day and just got back into town, so I guess I don't have my land legs back yet," I joke.

He still stays silent, but my words earn me a small smirk. That small rise at the corner of his mouth does things to me I'm not sure I like. His intense gaze settles on my face as if he's searching for something, and his lack of conversation has me shifting uncomfortably.

"Okay, well, I better get this stuff back to my parents. I'm in town to see them this week," I tell him, reaching for my cart. "Thank you again."

This time, he nods and touches the front of his hat before heading down the aisle.

I wrap up my shopping and head for the cashier to check out, sensing his eyes on me the whole time.

Who is this man?

Chapter 2

Dash

I find it amusing that she doesn't recognize me. I can't blame her. I look nothing like my former self with my long hair and thick beard. Not to mention the scar on my face.

My time in the military has changed not only my looks but also the man I used to be. Even my name is different, as I now go by Dash, which was my military nickname. The old version of me doesn't exist anymore.

Sky was my high school sweetheart—the girl I'll never forget. The one I never got over. She was and always will be the love of my life.

It's crazy to think I found her so early in life, but I wasn't ready for her then. I was stupid, and I walked away. I missed my chance with her, and I came to terms with that a long time ago. Still, she was the light during some of my darkest hours in the military.

This is the first time I've seen her since the day I left for boot camp. When I came home, I was worried about running into her but relieved to discover she'd moved and taken a job in Dallas.

She hasn't been home much since, even though her parents still live in town. It's easy to avoid her parents. I doubt they even know I'm back. We don't exactly run in the same circles.

But I can't deny those sparks when she crashed into me. Touching her after all this time had those feelings rushing back. Did she not feel them?

The more I think about it, the more I become irritated that she didn't recognize me. I shake my head. I'm a damn mess.

I continue shopping, keeping an eye on her as she fills her cart with all her favorite snacks. It's comforting to know some things haven't changed in all these years.

Her favorite cookies, chips, and ice cream make it into the basket before she heads to the checkout counter. I turn my back to the two girls, hoping to hear what they're saying—a little nugget to let me know she's okay. Just enough to keep me going.

"Any idea who he is?" Sky asks the cashier, who can't be more than eighteen.

I know she's talking about me. I'm the only other person in the store.

"No. He's in here every so often. He's always quiet and doesn't talk much, but they call him The Beast."

I frown. That damn nickname. I guess I've earned it from how I look, and it's spread, thanks to all the teenagers in town. I never tried to correct anyone. What's the point? If I tell them to stop, they'll simply do it behind my back.

"They shouldn't call him The Beast. He has a name. That you haven't learned his name says everything about you," Sky says as she takes the bag from the cashier, turns on her heel, and heads out the door.

There's that fiery temper I remember. When I turn to look at the cashier, her eyes are wide as she watches Sky walk out the door. She turns to me and sees me looking at her. I didn't think it was possible, but her eyes grow wider, and her face turns the brightest shade of red I've ever seen.

I turn away and continue shopping, trying to hide my huge smile. Sky may not have recognized me, but she stood up for me. She's still the fiery girl I fell in love with all those years ago.

I check out without saying a word. An awkward silence settles between the cashier and me, but she's polite and even smiles before I leave. People in town are always pleasant to my face. I can only imagine what they say behind my back.

I keep to myself, so it's probably more speculation than anything else. I don't correct anyone and let them believe what they want. Those who believe others' opinions without getting to know someone aren't worth my time.

I head home, and right before I pass my property line, I come across a car on the side of the road. Whoever's driving it is clearly from the city. The car itself isn't designed for country roads. It's tiny and has no power behind the engine. If I had to guess, it probably runs on electricity. I hope the driver didn't run out of juice because they won't find any place to charge the car out here.

I slow down as I approach the car. I may keep to myself, but I want to make sure the driver is okay. I roll down my passenger side window to find a female sitting behind the wheel. She looks over and gives me a shy smile before rolling down her window.

"You lost?" I inwardly cringe. I could've asked more politely, but not dealing with people regularly has made me forget how to talk to them.

"I don't think so. I stopped to answer a phone call and send in some information they needed for work." She holds up a folder, and I recognize the logo.

Wolf Land Development.

"And what do you do for them?" I ask, not wanting to play my hand just yet.

"Oh, I'm an assistant. The kind whose phone rings twenty-four-seven when they need something." She tries to laugh it off, but I detect an underlying discontent in her tone.

"A little word of advice. Your company isn't welcome around here. That big tree up there marks the start of my property line and where this becomes a private road. I suggest you turn around before you reach it." I tip my hat, roll my window up, and slowly pull away before she gets a chance to say anything else.

I get home and take a moment, standing in my front yard and looking up at the house where I now live. I grew up on this land and know it better than anyone. There are many large ranches like mine circling Walker Lake. This isn't the first time land developers have tried to snoop around, trying to get their hands on a ranch or two, throw up some developments, and turn this into a vacation town.

The residents here have no interest in it, and the ranchers will do anything to prevent it. However, this land development company has been a lot more persistent. They're causing problems, and they've racked up more trespassing charges than any development company before them.

And my gut tells me they're just getting started.

Chapter 3

Sky

The Beast has been on my mind since we ran into each other at the store last night. I can't shake the fact that he seems familiar, though I can't place him.

Still unable to get him off my mind, I decide to do a little digging. "Mom, what do you know about the man they call The Beast in town?"

My mom stops what she's doing and looks at me, her eyes wide with surprise before she quickly composes herself. "I know his name is Dash, but other than that, we know nothing about him. He's not very sociable, and we've never had a conversation with him. We only hear the whispers around town."

"And what is whispered around town?" I ask.

"Oh, you know, the usual things about how he's hardly ever out. They try to guess how he got the scar on his face and what he does all day." My mom waves her hand at me, dismissing the conversation, and returning to what she was doing.

I think about what my mom said. I get the feeling she isn't telling me something, but I believe her when she says they haven't talked or interacted. My parents don't much care for any of the ranchers and prefer to stick to the "lake people"—those who live on the lake and have money.

By lunch, I still can't get him out of my head, so I do the next best thing you can in a small town. I head in to have lunch at the diner and talk to Jenna and Austin.

Where Sarah and I have been friends since early elementary school, Jenna became friends with us over the past few years when Sarah was working with her at the diner. Austin and I became friends after she took over running the diner for her aunt.

I love that Jenna always greets you like you're the best friend she hasn't seen in years—and today is no different. You'd think I was a celebrity when I walked into the diner.

"Oh, my god, Sky! You're in town!" Jenna squeals, stopping what she's doing and running over to give me a huge hug.

This causes everyone in the diner to look my way, giving me small nods of acknowledgment. I grew up here, and most of them remember me from school or when I was in diapers.

"Please tell me you're going to stay for lunch. I'm due for a lunch break, and I would love to catch up," Jenna says when she finally pulls back and lets me breathe again.

"I plan on staying. I'm starving, and there are a few things I want to ask you about, if that's okay?"

"Of course! Grab a table. I'll put in our order, and we can chat when the food comes out."

I place my order without even looking at the menu. The food choices haven't changed in years, and everyone has their favorites.

As I wait for my food, I look around the place. It hasn't changed much since I was a kid. Austin has kept the traditional decor but has recovered the vinyl seats on all the chairs. The booths are still red, but they're all brand new.

The place is a lot cleaner than when Lee was running it. He was fired after he put his hands on Sarah, and Cal and his brothers stepped in. Turns out things ran a lot deeper than anyone thought, and he'd been stalking her with her parents' help. We have Ben to thank for helping to lock him up.

Sarah and I went to school with Ben, who's a cop. He owns a small house outside town, and he's done great things for Walker Lake.

I notice some new photos on the wall from around town. I'm pretty sure they're by Austin's sister, Natalie, who waited tables here until she married her husband.

"All right, here's our food. I can't even tell you what perfect timing this is. I'm starving. What did you want to know about?" Jenna asks.

"I was wondering about someone in town that I haven't seen before."

"Ask away, and I'll fill in any blanks I can," she says as she takes a big bite of her burger.

While Jenna eats, I fill her in on my trip to the grocery store yesterday and what the cashier said about "The Beast." I tell her he seemed vaguely familiar, but I couldn't place him, and I thought my mom was holding something back and didn't want me asking about him.

"It could all be in my head, but it has me curious as to who he is."

"You and everyone else in town, girl. I can tell you what I know for sure. He's new to town. Showed up a year ago and took over the Michaels ranch. The rest is speculation and gossip."

Damn. His working at the Michaels Ranch complicates things. I dated their son all through high school. I was so in love with him and certain we would end up together. Corey and I had great plans after high school, but then he joined the military and ended things.

I take a deep breath and push him out of my head. No point in going down that road.

"Any updates with the Michaels' son, Corey?" I ask, trying to figure out if I can even go to the ranch.

"I've never met him, but I haven't heard a word about him being home or anything other than what I know via you." Jenna shrugs and pushes her long, dark brown hair over her shoulder.

Austin appears and sits next to Jenna, stealing one of her fries. "Who are we gossiping about?"

"Who says we're gossiping?" Jenna pretends to be offended.

"Sky has her gossip face on. Besides, it's Walker Lake. Two girls together mean gossip. So, let's hear it," Austin says with a smile.

"Sky was asking about Dash. She ran into him at the store yesterday," Jenna explains, filling Austin in on our conversation.

"He took over the ranch not long after he came to town. The Michaels decided to retire and travel in an RV. They were in Maine last I heard," Austin says.

"And their son, Corey, isn't back from the military?" I ask, wanting to be sure.

Austin shrugs. "I haven't heard anything, and no one's mentioned him."

"But this Dash ... he's a nice guy?" I wonder out loud.

"I think so. He and Phantom have a bond. I see Dash petting him when they're in town together. Animals have the best sense of people," Austin says.

"Everyone always has nice things to say in here. He's helped a few of his neighbors deal with the land developers in town," Jenna adds.

I don't share my plans to go over and introduce myself later. I know they'll try to talk me out of it. Instead, I shift the topic to what I've missed around town since the last time I was here.

Things like the librarian, Candy, getting engaged to Ben's friend, North, over Christmas, and the family drama involved. What I wouldn't give to have been a fly on the wall for that one.

I spend the day with my parents and then make the excuse that I'm going to see a friend for dinner. I stop at the store and get what I need to make my meatloaf, mashed potatoes, green beans, and rolls. I also grab a cake from the tiny bakery section.

My nerves buzz the whole way to the Michaels ranch, and the butterflies in my stomach are intense. I made this drive many times in high school and always enjoyed it because it was relaxing and meant time with Corey.

I pull into the ranch and take a few deep breaths before approaching the familiar stone house.

I ring the bell and knock on the door the way I always did. A moment later, Dash opens the door and stands there, staring at me. He doesn't speak a word, and I rush to fill the silence.

"Remember me from the store yesterday?"

Dash nods.

"I asked around about you, and no one knows much. They say you keep to yourself, but I was wondering if I could make you dinner. I brought the ingredients to make meatloaf. This way, someone can say they gave you a proper Walker Lake welcome," I ramble.

A small, amused smile takes over his face, but he says nothing.

I wait for him to speak, but he keeps staring at me. So I stare right back, taking in his beard and the jagged scar on his cheek before looking him right in the eye.

Still, he says nothing.

"Do you talk?" I ask gently. Did the injury that gave him the scar also leave him mute?

"Yes." His voice is rough from lack of use.

"Do you want me to leave?" I continue once it's clear he won't say anything more.

"No."

That is all I get. "Okay. May I cook you dinner?" I ask politely.

"Yes."

I nod and return to my car, grabbing the bags of food from the store. When I turn to head to the house, I crash into a wall of pure muscle.

Those sparks are there again. They render me paralyzed for a moment before I take a step back and look into Dash's coffee-brown eyes. Eyes that I swear are familiar, but I still can't figure out where I know him from.

His chocolate-brown hair has a slight curl that peeks out from the cowboy hat on his head. Coffee and chocolate? I must be hungrier than I thought. Of course, that's the moment my stomach growls, breaking the silence between us.

Without a word, he takes the grocery bags from me and turns toward the house. Am I supposed to follow him? Did he change his mind? I watch him walk back to the house, his Wranglers hugging all the right places. The view is something to be appreciated. I'm debating what to do when he stops on the porch and looks back at me, catching my eyes on his gorgeous ass.

He nods his head toward the house, and that's all the encouragement I need to follow him inside.

This could be a very quiet supper.

Chapter 4

Dash

This girl. I haven't stopped thinking about her, and then she turns up on my front porch. Does she really not remember me? Maybe it's not an issue of remembering, but that she doesn't recognize me.

The last time I saw her, I was a scrawny rancher's kid. My head was shaved, and I didn't have facial hair or tattoos. Now, I have long hair, an unkempt beard, lots of tattoos, and muscles. Not to mention the ugly scar on the side of my face.

Yet Sky's here at the house she visited so many times. That means she must know, right?

"I used to come here all the time growing up. It's been so long since I've been here. They've kept it up so well," Sky says as she follows me to the kitchen, where I set the bags down.

Sky doesn't recognize me, but she hasn't forgotten me either. She must've asked around town about me. Seems people are saying nice enough things to make her feel comfortable coming here.

Sky smiles as she glances around the kitchen. Is she remembering the weekend my parents went out of town? I cooked her dinner, and we danced here in the kitchen. We got so lost in each other that I burned the hell out of the garlic bread. She laughed so hard and even tried to eat it, but it was unsavable.

"Is everything in the same place?" she asks, looking at me again.

I nod, worried the spell will be broken the moment I speak, and she'll run for the hills.

Sky sets to work, pulling out a mixing bowl and preheating the oven. "I'm making my meatloaf, which was always a favorite around here."

She spent many Saturdays making meatloaf with my mom, one of my favorite meals. Did she pick this meal because of her memories of me or the house?

I sit on a bar stool at the kitchen island and watch her move around the kitchen like I used to. Images of her doing this back then fill my head, and I start to get irritated. It reminds me of all the things I miss and the opportunity I wasted with her.

Why the hell doesn't she remember me? Do I really look so different with the overgrown hair and beard? She, of all people, should recognize me.

"I grew up in town. My parents own one of the lake houses, but I never fit in. I was always more at home on this ranch, working with the animals. Mrs. Michaels taught me so much; how to cook, clean, and save money. All the things I needed to live on my own, and my parents never bothered to show me."

The moment she starts speaking, all the anger bubbling inside me fades away, soothed by the sound of her voice.

"I left Walker Lake, went to school, kept my head down, and worked hard to graduate a year early. I didn't have much of a social life and didn't make any friends other than my roommate." She cringes. "I tried dating once, and it was so bad, I didn't do it again."

Whenever I thought about her in college, I imagined her going to parties, making friends, and having fun. I wanted her to be happy, even though the idea of her going on dates made me want to rip some imaginary guy's head off. That rage fueled my workouts, which helped advance my career—much good that did me.

"My parents worked their magic to get me a job at a start-up with some big-time tech guy. He's started up all these companies and made billions. I moved to Dallas and had a great little apartment downtown. I tried to convince myself I was living this great life. I liked my job, and I loved my coworkers. What more could I want?"

After mixing up the meatloaf, Sky moves to the sink to wash her hands. "Peace and fucking quiet. That's what I wanted. I hated the city and realized it even more when my friend Sarah married a guy who works on his family ranch in Rock Springs, Texas. I visited them, and it was so quiet. I had headaches for weeks when I went back to the apartment."

I know that feeling. Bootcamp was loud after growing up on the ranch. I went to bed many nights with my head in as much pain as my heart. Sky was on my mind every waking hour.

"You can imagine how relieved I was when the company started to go under. Only I couldn't find a job I liked. Then they cut my pay and handed me more work, so I quit. Put my stuff in storage and came home to visit for a week, hoping I could figure it out before I told my parents. It's not the first start-up this guy has failed, but I don't think my parents will care." She sighs. "Somehow, this will be my fault."

Part of me wants to gloat that the tables are finally turned, and she's not so high and mighty, but mostly my heart breaks for her. I know how her parents are, and I can see how much this is weighing on her. She has bags and dark circles under her eyes, and she's paler than she should be.

"I wish I could stay here in town. I want to come home, but all the jobs I find are in the city. Sarah has offered me to let me stay with her and work on the ranch. I love the idea, but Rock Springs isn't home like Walker Lake."

Sky puts dinner in the oven and starts on the sides. Once they're going, she looks up and gives me a shy smile.

"Sorry for dumping all that on you. I have a habit of filling the silence, and I guess I needed to get that all off my chest more than I realized."

I like the idea of her staying in town, and an idea forms in my head as she talks about the job she left in Dallas.

"Okay, now we let it cook," Sky says, washing her hands and turning to me.

"Would you like a tour of the ranch?" I ask, my voice gruff. That's what happens when you don't talk much.

Her eyes widen for a second. Is it because I spoke? Or has she finally realized who I am?

Then, the expression is gone, and she smiles. "I'd like that."

I give her a quick house tour. My mom has re-decorated since Sky was last here, so things look different. My dad said it gave Mom something to focus on instead of how much danger I could be in.

I thought I'd walked into the wrong house when I came home from training. But she made some upgrades that I'm now thankful for.

"This place is so different from the last time I was here. Corey went off to boot camp right after we graduated, and I haven't been back here since. I bet his mom needed to take her mind off him. I know I sure did. It's why I threw myself into my studies."

Once the house tour is done, we head outside to see the barn, but Sky stops at the door. This is where I ended things between us, and it took me a while before I could come back here, too.

On the way back to the house, I take her to the rose garden I started when I got home. It's where I go to get away, and no one bothers me out here. It gives me something to do when my mind wanders.

"Roses are my favorite, and these are so beautiful," she says in awe as we walk into the gated garden.

Sky loved roses and always smelled of them from her shampoo and perfume. Roses make me think of her.

We head inside, and I set the table as she gets the food ready and on the table—a table I haven't used once since I've been home since it's been only me. I eat at the kitchen island or in front of the TV. Dinner was at the table when I was growing up. There may have been other people in and out, but we ate at the table as a family.

Sky keeps the conversation going through dinner, and I only interject a word or two now and again. She doesn't seem to mind my minimal contribution. She tells me about things in town, her friends, and her life in Dallas. I ask her a question here or there to keep her talking, and she seems happy to do so.

She looks me in the eyes and doesn't stare at my scar. I'm sure she must be curious. Everyone is. But she doesn't ask, and we don't talk about my military time, which is nice to not think about. She lets me just be me. That's something I've been missing for a long time now.

Much as I enjoy her company, I remind myself that the issues we faced back then are still there. Her family has money. They're cash rich. My parents are land rich. In this town, that's what divides people.

It was too much back then and will be our downfall now. She'll tire of things out here, eventually. Maybe it's time I show her that.

Chapter 5

Sky

I'm nervous when we sit down to eat dinner. I know I can cook a meatloaf because I learned how to cook it in this kitchen all those years ago. But I'm nervous to see if Dash will like it, and that's new for me.

He doesn't say much at dinner, he just lets me talk, but he clears his plate three times. I can't sit in silence, so I talk about people in town I've run into since being back, the changes at the diner, and how I can't wait to sneak away to the library. Then I tell him all about my job and how I'm not only unemployed but also homeless.

He listens to me ramble and asks a few questions, letting me know he's at least listening and I'm not driving him too crazy. When dinner is over, he helps clear the table and insists on doing the dishes himself. I don't know many cowboys who will do dishes—they're usually on to the next thing that needs to be done when dinner is over.

"Thank you. That was the best meal I've had since being here," Dash says.

I can tell by the look in his eyes he means it. "I'm glad I could show you some real Walker Lake hospitality."

"I was thinking..." He trails off, almost like he doesn't want to ask the question.

"Yes?" I encourage.

"I need some help around here. Cooking and cleaning. The pay isn't much, but I can cover your room and board. There's an apartment above the garage. I can take you there to see it." He doesn't look at me as he says it.

Did he just offer me a job and a place to live?

Holy shit.

It's not my dream job, but I can cook and clean, and it's on a ranch, which I know I'll love. It gives me a place to live for the time being, and I'm sure I can find a way to spin this to appease my parents. Maybe something like they closed the office, so I work for Dash for room and board.

"Do you want to see the apartment? It's not much, but I think you'll like it," Dash says, breaking me from my thoughts.

I can worry about my parents later. I just got here. I have at least a week before they start asking questions. "Yes, please."

He nods and turns to head out the back door. I follow him hesitantly because I don't remember an apartment above the garage the last time I was here. Of course, that was many years ago.

I follow him up the stairs to the side of the garage and can't help but admire the view of his Wrangler-clad butt. I shake my head. I can't go there when he's nice enough to offer me a job and a place to stay.

When I step into the apartment, I pause, taken aback. It's like stepping into a space chosen from my personal home design folder. A small bedroom and bathroom are on one side, with an open-plan living room, dining, and kitchen on the other.

The walls are light gray, and the floor is wood. There are wood accents everywhere, in the beams and floating shelves. The couch and the dining chair cushions add splashes of dark pink and red.

The furniture is basic, with a table, chairs, a couch, and a bed. All the place needs is the small stuff like plates, decorations, and my clothes—all of which I have.

"This is beautiful. Can I think about it and get back to you?" I ask, not wanting to commit to moving in with a stranger, no matter how badly I want to take this chance.

Dash nods. "Of course."

He's a perfect gentleman and walks me to my car, thanking me again for the meal. The moment I turn onto the main road, I call Sarah.

"How was dinner?" she asks.

Sarah is the one person who knows everything. She's my best friend in the whole world and has known me the longest. I can't remember a day when we haven't talked, even if only by text.

"It went well. Too good, maybe?" I say, trying to figure out my feelings.

"Sky! You did not sleep with him!" Sarah gasps.

I almost drop the phone. "What? No! Good lord!" I laugh because her mind went there.

When you have a husband like Mac, who looks like a hero and puts in the work for you, I'm sure she gets laid every night. Sex is always on her brain.

"Oh, thank God. So, what happened?"

I tell her about dinner on the drive back to town, what Dash and I talked about, and finally, the job offer.

"So, what do you think?" I ask once I'm done.

"I can tell you want to take the job. I just don't know why. Is it solely because you don't want to tell your parents what is going on?"

I sigh. "I think it's more that I don't want to deal with my parents once I tell them."

"But that isn't a reason to take the job. You can stay here as long as you need, you know that. What's the real reason?"

I pull into the county park before making the drive along the lake to my parents' house. What *is* the real reason?

"Honestly, Walker Lake is my home, and I have wanted to come back for a while now. Not to my parents, but to the town."

"So you want to take it," Sarah states.

It's not a question, but I answer anyway. "Yes."

"What do you know about this man? Did Corey's parents sell the land to him?"

"No, he's taken over running it for them since Corey is off playing GI Joe. But I don't know much other than they call him The Beast, but his real name is Dash. He was nothing but polite and nice when I was there."

"If the Michaels trust him to run their ranch, he must be a good person. I don't know anything about him, but I'm a bit out of the loop. Have you talked to Jenna?"

"Yeah, and Austin. They don't know much."

"I think you should talk to Ben. Since he's a cop, he'll be honest with you about what you should do, and if he doesn't know, he'll dig," Sarah advises.

She's right. Having a cop as a friend is never a bad thing. He helped Sarah when she needed it, and I know he'll be straightforward with me.

"If Ben says he's all right, I think you should do it," Sarah adds.

We catch up a bit more before saying goodbye, and I give Jenna a quick call to update her too.

"Ben has lunch at the diner almost every day during the week. You could stop by and chat with him. It's less formal than going down to the station," Jenna says.

I pout. "But everyone will hear, and they won't keep that news to themselves."

Jenna laughs. "What do you think the gossip will be if you're seen walking into the station and disappearing behind a closed door with Ben? The stories will be wild. Everything from you're secretly dating to you're working undercover on the same case."

She's right. It's worse to let the town wonder. The longer something goes without answers, the wilder the town rumor mill becomes. Look at how they've handled Dash.

"Okay. I'll be there for lunch tomorrow," I relent.

"Perfect, see you then!"

I end the call and finally finish the drive home.

"How was dinner with Jenna, dear?" my mom asks when I walk in the door.

I used Jenna as my cover, and she was all too happy to help. My parents like her because her family also owns a house on the lake—only Jenna's parents don't care about the divide between the town and love the ranchers. They're sweet and helpful and don't give their kids handouts.

Jenna's brothers have been working their butts off to save up to buy a ranch for the three of them to run together. Jenna's parents could have handed them the ranch, but it wouldn't have meant nearly as much as them earning it.

They've started looking around to see if they can find a deal, but it'll probably be a few more years before they get anything.

"Dinner was good. It was good to catch up. I miss Jenna when I'm in Dallas. I wish I could make friends like her and Sarah there," I tell Mom honestly.

I felt isolated in Dallas. I tried to make friends and was on good terms with the people I worked with. We went out to dinner or drinks, but I never made any good friends. No one I want to keep in contact with now that I won't be going back.

"You need to get out more. Volunteer work is a great way to make friends, dear," Mom says.

I nod, not bothering to tell her I had no time to volunteer when I worked seventy-hour weeks. I know I won't win that argument.

I go to my room and plop down on my bed. I can't believe my life has come down to debating if I can trust a stranger's job offer and move in with him.

Where did I go wrong?

Chapter 6

Sky

I head into town to have lunch with Jenna. My parents were up early for some event in Amarillo. I honestly wasn't paying attention as they droned on about the need to save some birds.

My short drive into the diner makes me realize this town hasn't changed a bit in the eight years since I went off to college and got a job in Dallas. The houses on the lake are still perfectly manicured. The county park still has young mothers with their kids on the playground and dog owners who run with their dogs every morning on the jogging trail near the lake.

The faces might have changed, but it's still Walker Lake, a small town with a big divide between those on the lake and those on the ranches. The one thing that seems to bring everyone together is Phantom, standing in front of the city hall, surrounded by little kids petting him.

The town spoils the horse, and he loves it. He's so good with little kids when they want to pet him or get a picture with him. He keeps looking toward the diner, where he'll get fed by Austin. She'll give him a few extra treats today for sure.

I park and head into the diner where, sure enough, Austin is watching Phantom out the front window with a huge smile on her face. The bell jingles as I walk in, pulling her attention from the window.

"Sky! Perfect timing. Jenna is due for a break." She gives me a quick hug before disappearing out the back.

A moment later, Jenna appears, removing her apron. "Let's sit here. I already put our food order in, and Austin said she'll bring it out when it's ready." Jenna drops her apron in a booth and goes to the counter to grab our drinks. "Ben should be here soon. The only time he's late is when he gets a call."

Chances are, Ben will be here like usual. It's rare for there to be a call during lunchtime. Everyone is eating, and with it being a small town, if it isn't urgent, they let the cops like Ben eat before answering a call.

Not a moment later, the bell over the door jingles and Ben enters wearing full uniform. If this were some fancy movie, the sunlight would frame the doorway as he removed his sunglasses, women would swoon, and he'd give all the girls a cocky smile.

But this isn't a movie, and when he walks in, Phantom gives him a hard nudge from behind, causing the diners to laugh as his sunglasses drop to the ground. He picks them up, and Jenna flags him over as Austin takes a large bowl of goodies out to Phantom.

"Hello, ladies," Ben says, removing his hat and sitting next to Jenna.

"Hey, Ben. Sky wanted to ask your opinion on something," Jenna starts.

Austin comes back in, gets Ben a drink, and brings it to the table. "The usual?" she asks.

"Yes, ma'am." He smiles, and Austin blushes before heading off to put in his order. Ben turns to me. "I'm all ears."

"It's about Dash." I make sure none of the church ladies can overhear before I tell Ben I cooked dinner for Dash and about his job offer.

Our food is served, and Ben takes a few bites of the BBQ ribs he ordered while thinking about what to say. "Dash is a good guy. He's quiet and keeps to himself, which allows some people in town to make up what they want about him. He doesn't care what people think, but he doesn't hear most of it, so he doesn't correct it. Like his nickname, The Beast."

I cringe. The nickname sounds so harsh compared to the man I spent time with.

"I know you stood up for him at the store when the cashier used that nickname. Outside of Jenna, Austin, and me, you're the only person who's stood up for him and gone out of your way to get to know him."

Ben takes a few more bites of his burger while that sets in. I find it sad that Dash is treated like an outsider in a small town that protects its own.

"He's the first one there when someone needs help. His neighbors had a fire last year, not long after he moved here, and he helped them rebuild, no questions asked. He wasn't talkative and kept to himself, but he was the hardest worker there." Ben points a French fry at me as if trying to get his point across.

"I remember that. Austin had me bring lunch for the volunteers there, and Dash didn't even like to stop to eat. Some of the other guys tried to talk to him and include him in the conversations, but he wanted nothing to do with it. He just kept working," Jenna says.

"So, if I take this job, I won't end up chained in the basement or chopped up in his freezer?" I ask Ben to be sure.

He picks up his burger to take a bite to hide his smile.

"What are you hiding, Ben?" I ask as I sit back in the booth and cross my arms over my chest.

"Dash is a nickname, is all. But he's a good person, and you'll be safe there. Honestly, you'll be safer there than with your parents, but I'll deny I ever said that."

I still suspect Ben's hiding something, but I decide not to press. I know Ben, and he won't tell me anything if he doesn't want to.

We finish up lunch by talking a bit about the land developers and who they've been harassing. We all agree that we wish they'd take the hint and go away. No one wants them here, and no one is going to sell to them, but they aren't the sharpest tools in the tool shed.

After lunch, I head down to my storage unit and sort through what I'll need to take with me if I take the job with Dash. I want to, but I need time to ensure I'm okay with it.

I pull aside boxes of dishes, blankets, photos, and my clothes. I didn't keep a lot of furniture, just a few of my favorite items, like the coffee table I got at the thrift store, my comfortable mattress, my TV, and a few lamps I love. I sold everything else because I figured I could replace it when the time came.

After a few hours, I'm pretty sure I want to take the job, so I load a few things into the trunk of my car and head over to talk to Dash.

Chapter 7

Sky

I'm on my way from the barn to the house when I hear a car coming up the driveway.

Great. The last thing I want to deal with is company, and chances are, it's a land developer again. I need to get the gate fixed and start locking it. I can't remember the last time my family had to do that, or anyone in Walker Lake, for that matter.

I walk into the house and grab my shotgun before opening the front door to greet whoever is there, shocked to find Sky getting out of her car. I set the shotgun down on the porch as I watch her get out of her car and hesitantly walk up to the porch where I'm standing.

"Is that job offer still on the table?" she asks, looking up at me.

"It is," I tell her and cross my arms.

She stands tall. "I'd like to take it."

"Then it's yours." I turn and grab a key ring from the hook on the wall. "These are your keys to the apartment, the house, and the gate. Let me know when you want to move your stuff in, and I'll make sure you have help."

She takes the keys from me. "I have a few things in my car now. I need to go pack up the stuff at my parents'. I can start in the morning if that's okay?"

"That's fine. I'll cook tonight, and you're welcome to join me. I'll help with the stuff in your car now."

She backs her car up to the apartment steps, and we unload a few boxes. I was expecting a lot more, but the apartment is well-furnished, and I remember her saying she'd given up her place in Dallas.

"I have space in the garage if you want to store any furniture, so you don't have to pay for a storage unit," I offer.

I like having her here even though I don't think I should. I need to keep my distance and enjoy her being around.

Neither of us talks as we unload her boxes into the apartment. Several times, I catch Sky watching me, but she doesn't say anything until we've finished unloading all the boxes.

"Thank you for your help. It made things much easier," she says.

I nod, and she follows me back outside. I catch her looking at me again, which reminds me of the times I caught her gazing at me from across a classroom or down the hall when she was talking to her friends. She's studying me like she did all those years ago. I loved the feeling of her eyes on me back then, and I love it now.

"Have we met before? I swear you look familiar, but I can't place you," she says thoughtfully.

I shrug and turn to head toward the house without a word.

"I'm sorry. I'm going to grab my stuff from my parents'. I'll be back in a bit."

I nod again and head inside. I watch her leave before going inside to start dinner. Day one, and already, things aren't going to plan. I need to keep my distance, which I know will be easier said than done.

Keeping my distance was something I could never do with Sky. She pulled me to her, no matter where I was. I was always calmer and happier when I was near her. That still seems to be the case.

I'm making dinner when there's a knock on the back door. No one knocks here—the ranch hands just walk in if they need anything.

I open the door hesitantly to find Sky there. "No one knocks on that door. You live here, so just come on in," I tell her as I return to cooking dinner.

"That will take some getting used to," she says as she looks around.

What memories does she recall as she looks around the kitchen? Is it the many afternoons she spent cooking with my mom? Or maybe it's the times we sat in the living room watching a movie or reading on the couch when we were on break from school.

The furniture may be new, but it's still in the same place, so it's easy to recall my favorite memories, all of which contain Sky.

"What happened to the Michaels who owned this place before?" she asks, shattering the memories.

Her question reminds me that she still doesn't know who I am. "I run it now," I answer abruptly before changing the subject. "We'll need a menu plan so I can get what you need. I'll send a guy into Amarillo to do a bulk stock-up. We converted part of the garage into a room for food storage. There are several freezers, a huge pantry, and an extra stove and fridge if needed."

I can feel her eyes on me as I stir the sauce on the stove. I don't want to lie to her, but if she hasn't figured it out by now, it's not my problem. Right?

"This will take half an hour in the oven. How about I give you a better tour and explain your duties while we wait?" I finally turn to face her.

She studies me for a moment before nodding and standing.

"I've been using the pantry, fridge, and freezer to store meals for the next few days, along with snacks and such. There's a menu plan printed on the fridge for the guys, but I keep a list on the computer too. It's easier for whoever runs into town next. I'll get you set up on the computer tomorrow. Let me show you the garage and where I keep the keys.

The garage is locked to keep out animals that may smell the food.

"We keep lesser-used things in here too. Depending on how you cook, you can move them inside and other things out of here. This will be your domain." I look at the things of my mom's that I had no idea how to use but didn't have the heart to get rid of.

"Oh, good. The big slow cooker is out here. That will be great to use, especially on hot days."

Sky knows more about all this stuff than I do. Mom taught me to cook, but it was never my job to cook for everyone on the ranch until now. I'm more than happy to hand that job over to

Sky. I'd rather feed the animals in the barn than the humans on this ranch.

"It will be your job to keep everyone on the ranch fed—breakfast, lunch, and supper. Breakfast should be grab-and-go. You'll need to plan something easy for lunch you can bring out to the field and also have here at the house. Everyone comes in to grab their food at dinner and takes it wherever they choose to eat."

"I can handle that. Are there any food allergies or things to avoid?"

"We don't do fancy city food here. We're meat and potato eaters. No allergies, no vegetarians. Meals should be filling and taste good. The classics are best."

"I can do that," Sky says with a smile and a nod.

"You're also in charge of cleaning the main living areas, the bathroom, and your apartment. The men take care of their spaces. I'll handle my bedroom, bathroom, and office. Let's head out to the barn, and I'll introduce you to a few of the men."

The walk out to the barn is silent but not uncomfortable. There are only two men there, and I introduce them to Sky. She's polite but gravitates to the horses in the barn, who seem to love her.

"You're free to ride in your free time. Just ask one of the guys. They'll know which horse you can use and the equipment for you. Some horses need to be exercised, and others need rest, so always ask."

"I will. I promise," she says, petting my mom's horse, Hershey.

Mom named her because her coat is the color of a chocolate bar. Hershey has always favored females over males and will get along great with Sky. My mom won't mind her riding Hershey, but I make a mental note to check with her to be sure.

Sky steps back from the stall and stumbles as she hits a patch of uneven ground. I wrap an arm around her waist to catch her, and the same sparks from the store the other day erupt across my skin—the ones I always experienced when we were dating.

They haven't gone away, no matter how much time has passed. I always thought I exaggerated them and that they were part of the whole teenage hormone thing because I haven't felt them since. Until I held Sky again.

"Sorry. I promise I'm not usually this clumsy." Sky takes a step away from me.

I know she isn't clumsy, but it sure looks like it the past few days. Of course, a lot has changed between us, so for all I know, she lost her sense of balance in the city.

I shake my head. "It's fine."

We return to the house, and Sky walks so close to me that our arms touch now and then. When we round the last corner to the house, Phantom is standing in the middle of the walkway to greet us.

"Oh, hey, buddy. I didn't know you came out this far." Sky walks up to him and hugs him before petting him.

"Yeah, he comes out here. We have an open stall for him to sleep in. He gets food, and the other horses love him. Go on into the barn, buddy. They'll get you some food," I tell Phantom.

Almost like he understands me, he nods and brays before walking to the barn behind us. I turn to Sky to find her smiling at me—the same smile that used to make me feel a thousand feet tall. I lived for that smile.

It kept me going on the battlefield, even when I thought I'd never see it again.

Is there any chance there could be more between us again?

I'm pretty sure that ship has sailed and burned. I was the one who burned it.

But a man can always hope.

Chapter 8

SKY

It's been a few days, and Dash has been in to eat every meal with me. Breakfast is grab-and-go, but he still eats with me. Dash talks about what's happening on the ranch that day, and I share what's going on in town. It's easy conversation and something Corey's parents used to do.

The ranch hands are in and out while we eat, and I've gotten to know each of them. They're friendly but don't hang out in the house for long. They grab food, say hello and talk for a minute before heading outside.

They're getting comfortable putting in meal requests with me, and so far, it's been simple things like meatloaf and pot roast. One guy asked me to make his mom's chicken with chili and said he'd get me the recipe. I'm excited about that one. Chili is popular around here on a cold day.

I still can't shake the feeling that I know Dash from somewhere, but I have no idea where. It keeps me up at night, trying to place him. It's on the edge of my memory, but when I get close, it disappears. I hope I figure it out soon.

The few times I bring it up, Dash shuts down and changes the subject. I like what we have now, and I don't want to push it and risk messing things up.

Once Dash leaves for the morning, I start on lunch and supper. Then, I clean until lunchtime and use my time between lunch and dinner to learn my way around the ranch again.

I go riding on Hershey, and we have a great time. She loves to be out on the ranch and knows her way around. I let her pick where to go, and she took me to a little pond I didn't even know was here. It's so peaceful and the perfect place to lay out a blanket to read and enjoy some peace and quiet.

I think about asking Dash if he knows the spot, but I like having a place on the ranch that's just mine.

Hershey seems to enjoy the spot, too. She's very relaxed and grazes on what little grass there is at this time of year. I wish I could spend all day being lazy, reading, and enjoying what's left of the good weather before things turn cold.

We head back to the barn much sooner than I'd like. I give Hershey freedom, and she takes me on a different path home than we took to the little pond area. Many people see the flat Texas landscape this far north as boring, but I think the wide-open fields of the ranches are some of the most beautiful scenery you'll ever see.

Come spring; these fields will be full of bluebonnets and wildflowers so vibrant they'll light up the Texas landscape. That view beats any mountain, river, or beach. And if I want to see water or stick my toes in the sand, all I have to do is go down to the lake. It's the best of both worlds.

As I get closer to the house, I start to get notifications on my phone. I don't have service as I get further from the house, which is part of the draw of going for a ride. I check the notifications to see that Sarah has called and listen to her voicemail to see what's going on.

"Hey, girl. I'm just checking in and making sure you're doing okay. I know you're getting settled in to your new job, but I figured someone should check on you to make sure Dash is the good guy everyone says he is. Give me a call back. We're making plans to head up to the lake in the next few weeks."

I've got a bit of time before returning to the house to start dinner, so I call Sarah to set her mind at ease.

"At least you're not dead, so there's that. How is the job going?"

"The job is good. Being on this ranch without his family is a weird feeling, but I get the afternoons to go riding, which is what I was doing when you called. I didn't have service. Everybody's friendly and laid back. All in all, it's a pretty easy job."

"I always figured you'd end up on a ranch instead of in the city. Have you thought about what comes after since I know you were planning on this only being temporary?"

"To be honest, I haven't even given it a thought or started looking. I think I need some time to decompress. I'm not sure if I want to get back into the tech world or find something a little closer to home."

"Take your time. Don't rush into anything," Sarah advises. "So, how's your boss?"

"Better than I expected." I can't help but smile when I say that.

"I can tell there's something there. You're not falling for him, are you?" Sarah asks in a slightly teasing voice laced with concern.

"He's not anything like I expected. He sits and has breakfast and dinner with me. He doesn't talk much but asks questions and listens when I talk. It makes me think the town giving him The Beast nickname is based solely on his long hair, beard, and scar.

It seems unfair because he's a good guy if people would take the time to get to know him."

"You know as well as anybody that it goes both ways. He has to be willing to let people in, and that's not always the case. Just be careful."

"Oh, I am. When are you guys thinking of coming up to the lake?" I change the subject, and thankfully she lets me.

"We're starting to make plans. Is there a time that works better for you?"

"Not really. My schedule is wide open other than work."

"Okay, good. We'll get some plans together, and I'll let you know."

We chat for a bit longer about what's going on with her and in Rock Springs until I reach the barn and say goodbye.

I pass Hershey to one of the ranch hands, who'll take care of her and give her a good brush down.

I head inside to start on dinner, surprised to find Dash sitting at the dining room table with papers spread out.

"I'm sorry. I have to get these taken care of and mailed out, and then I'll be out of your way," he says.

"Take your time. You're not in my way," I tell him as I remove my shoes and prepare to cook.

I get dinner going, and we both work in comfortable silence. Neither of us seems inclined to fill it with needless conversation.

Dinner is almost ready when there's a loud knock on the door. I look at Dash, who's looking at me. Neither of us is expecting company.

Dash grabs the shotgun on the way to the door while I stay in the kitchen. I can't see the front door from here, but I can hear the general tone of the conversation, and there's no mistaking that Dash is angry. It's only when his voice rises that I can hear every word.

"I've told you and the people who work with you I'm not interested in selling and to stay off my property. This is the last time I'll be polite about it. Next time, I'll be shooting a hello because you're now considered trespassers. Spread the word. You have sixty seconds to get off my land."

The only sound is Dash pumping the shotgun. I can't see what's happening, but I hope the unwanted visitor is running for his car. A moment later, the front door closes, and I turn to face Dash.

When he sees me, his eyes go wide, almost like he forgot I was here.

· · · • · • • · · ·

Dash

I watch the guy scramble to his car faster than I thought possible for someone in such expensive shoes. If I weren't so pissed that he was trespassing on my land, I'd find it comical how he shoves everything into his car and heads down the driveway without even putting his seatbelt on.

I turn and head inside, only to be faced with Sky.

"Who was that?" she asks.

Shoot, I forgot she was standing there. I didn't want her to see me like this; like The Beast everyone claims I am.

"A land developer is trying to buy up the Silver Cattle Ranch. The owner won't sell to them, even though he's looking for a buyer. They've been hounding his neighbors, me included. Those guys are snakes and don't care about what's good for the town, and they'll play dirty to get what they want. I've seen their kind before."

Sky steps forward and places her hand on my arm, instantly calming me. This could be dangerous.

"My friend, Ben, who I went to school with, is a cop. He was telling me about the land developers and the trouble the Ranchers are having because of them. Hopefully, they'll get tired and move on to another town that may want to give up their land and let them destroy it."

Of course, she gets it. She grew up here and listened when my dad talked about the developers who'd tried in the past. Though, back then, they would move on if people said no.

"We can only hope. Let me clean off the table, and I'll help you finish dinner."

Thankfully, Sky takes the bait and understands I want to change the subject.

I clean off the paperwork I've been working on all afternoon and put it in my office. Returning to the kitchen, I help Sky set the table and prepare everything for the ranch hands to come in and grab their food.

"Whatever you're cooking smells good," I tell her as she puts the final touches on the food.

"Thanks. I went for a classic. Chicken and dumplings."

Even though the kitchen is a decent size, we keep brushing against each other, which drives me crazy. At one point, Sky looks up at me with a smile, and the desire to kiss her is so overwhelming I have to leave the room. I want her to know it's me when she kisses me. The problem is, I'm not sure I'm brave enough to tell her.

Chapter 9

SKY

The next day, I'm at the diner on my day off when I run into Ben again.

"Damn, you're here almost as much as I am." He greets me with a smirk that I'm sure drives other girls crazy, but it's not my style.

"Yes, one of the perks of staying in town and having one of your best friends working here. But I'm glad I ran into you. Can I ask you another question?"

"Sure. Let's grab this booth and get our food in before the lunch rush," he says, leading us to a booth at the side of the restaurant.

"You both want your usuals?" Jenna comes over the moment our butts hit the vinyl seats.

I let it sink in that not only do people know me, but I also have a usual at the diner. I often visited my favorite coffee shop or the little cafe around the corner from my apartment in Dallas, and

I never had anyone remember me, much less my order. It was partly because the city is so big and partly because turnover in those positions was pretty high.

"Yes, that sounds perfect," I tell Jenna.

"Sounds good to me, too," Ben says.

"I wanted to ask about the land developers a bit more."

"What about them?" he asks, his steady gaze giving nothing away.

"One showed up yesterday, and Dash was angry and upset. He told him he wouldn't give them any more warnings, and the next time they'd be considered trespassers and shot on sight. It's the first time I've seen him upset at anything, so I wondered how big of a problem they've been."

"Every few years, we have developers sniffing around. They get told no, and they're gone within a month or two. These guys are sticking around like a nasty rash. No matter how many people turn them down, they're still here and getting too persistent," Ben replies, obviously choosing his words carefully.

"In other words, they're getting mean and sneaky?" I cut to the truth.

"They're heading that way. They've trespassed on ranches, and there's no reason for it unless their intentions are questionable. Sadly, there isn't much I can do because they haven't been caught breaking any laws ... yet."

"I know you'll do what you can. All you can do is notify the ranchers and let everyone know you're here if they need you," I try to reassure him.

"I never realized how much getting into law enforcement tied my hands to preventing crimes. We're there after they happen, not to stop them, and I hate that," he grumbles as Jenna delivers our food.

We're silent for a few minutes as we tuck into our food.

"So, how's the new job working out?" Ben cuts his eyes toward the table near the door with all the gossiping church ladies.

"I haven't told my parents, so please don't tell anyone," I whisper.

He shrugs and digs into his fries. "I have no reason to tell anyone."

"Otherwise, it's going well. I have most afternoons free, and I've been going riding again. It's good to have a slower-paced job."

We talk for a bit longer, and as we finish, Ben eyes the table by the door. "You won't get by that table without a million questions about why you're still in town. I'll distract them."

"Ben—"

"Consider it a thank you for helping Dash. He's a good guy, and not many people would give him a chance like you have." Ben pays the bill before heading toward the door and letting the church ladies suck him in.

I stand and try to make a run for it, but I'm not so lucky.

"Oh, Sky, dear. Is it true you took a job working for The Beas—I mean, Dash?" Mrs. Riley asks.

I look at Ben, who shakes his head slightly, indicating he hasn't told anyone. But of course, it could have been anyone from one of the ranch hands to Dash himself who let it slip I was working there.

"I am while I'm in town." I smile and take another step toward the door when I'm assaulted with questions and unwanted comments from the group.

"Is it true he has bars on the door and windows?"

"Is he pining away all day for some lost love?"

"I bet his horses are scared of him."

"I heard no one is allowed to leave the ranch, and he keeps everyone gated in."

"I heard he's on the run, and the scar is a fake."

All the ladies talk at once, and I can't keep up.

"I can assure you there are no bars on the windows and doors, his animals aren't scared of him, and he works as hard as his ranch hands. Here I am on my day off, living proof that he doesn't gate us in. And why in the world would you think his scar is fake?"

I don't wait for an answer, forcing my way outside before any more questions are tossed my way. I feel a little bad for bailing on Ben, and I'll apologize to him later, although I'm sure he understands.

As I turn the corner and head to my car, I run into Phantom.

"Hey there, boy. Where did you come from?" I lean in and pet him.

"The secrets he could tell if he could talk," Dash says from behind me.

"Hey, Dash. What are you doing here?" I ask as I continue to pet Phantom.

"Needed a few things to fix up one of the gates," he replies, giving Phantom a good scratch.

"Well, I'd avoid the diner. They're gossiping about you and cornered me since they found out I'm working for you," I warn him.

His expression doesn't change, but I see something I can't make out in his eyes. Hurt maybe? Anger? I'm not sure.

I sigh. "I tried to correct a few of the rumors, but some are crazy."

He gives me a small smile. "Thanks, but correcting one rumor will only start five more. Let them talk."

"They make up gossip because you're so mysterious. Talking to them for five minutes would quell some of that gossip."

"Maybe. Be safe getting back to the ranch, and enjoy your day off." He tips his hat and heads into the town square.

I look at Phantom. "I'm beginning to think you show up when all the drama is about to happen so you can watch," I tell him.

He nods like he's agreeing with me and heads into the town square after Dash.

Chapter 10

Dash

I decide to check the fence lines as a precaution after the land developer's visit, but also because it helps to take my mind off Sky. She's on my mind from the moment I wake up until I go to bed. I can't seem to escape her, even in my dreams.

I appreciated how she defended me in the diner yesterday and warned me about what I might be walking into. I took her advice and avoided the diner, but I still felt eyes on me as I walked past. Sure enough, all the town gossips were staring out the window at me. Lord knows what they're saying now that Sky is working for me.

Yesterday was her day off, but she still came home and cooked dinner, which allowed us to keep our usual dinner talk going. I still can't process why I was relieved not to miss a day with her.

I'm so lost in thought I almost jump out of my skin when a cold nose brushes against my arm. I turn to see Phantom looking at me, almost as if he's asking if I'm okay.

"Sorry, buddy. Just lost in thought," I tell him, reaching out to pet him.

He leans down to sniff at my jeans pocket, where I tend to keep a few treats in case we run into each other.

"You hungry?" I ask, pulling out a little snack for him. He eats it while I check the time. "Shoot, I'm going to be late for dinner. Time got away from me today. You know where the barn is," I tell him, packing up my tools and heading back to the barn.

"Better hurry. Sky made tacos, and I doubt there will be leftovers," Drake, one of my ranch hands, says.

I already feel bad for being late, but I'll feel horrible if I miss dinner altogether. I put my stuff away and hand my horse off to Drake before high-tailing it up to the house.

"Just in time!" Sky says when she sees me coming through the door, already eating at the table.

I make a plate and sit down with her. "I'm sorry I'm late. Time got away from me today."

"It's okay. I know not everything on a ranch runs by a clock." She smiles as she repeats what my dad said so many times growing up.

"You're right, but I try to be here unless it's completely unavoidable."

We talk over dinner. Well, Sky talks, and I listen. Mostly she tells me about a new TV show she's started watching. It's so cute how excited she gets over a two-year-old TV show she finally has time to watch. She tells me about her seventy-hour work weeks in Dallas and how she never had time to do anything other than work, sleep, and drink coffee to keep her going.

After dinner, I stay and help with the dishes, partly because I feel bad but mostly because I want to spend more time with her since I was late back.

Other than meal prep for tomorrow, Sky is off the clock once the dishes are done. She usually heads to her apartment to watch TV or read as the rest of us finish our nighttime chores before turning in for the night.

"You don't have to help with dishes. I know you have things to do before bed." She smiles and takes a plate from me that I cleared from the table.

Our fingers brush, and we both freeze. That sensation is there again; this time, I'm certain she feels it too. Our eyes lock, and time stands still. I don't know how long we stand there, but we're pulled back to reality when the screen door slams shut behind a ranch hand coming in to grab food late.

The spell is broken, but the feelings are still there. I turn back to the table and clean off the last few dishes before grabbing a towel to dry what she washes. We have a dishwasher, but with feeding the ranch hands, it doesn't hold everything, so hand-washing dishes is a nightly chore.

Neither of us talks as she washes dishes and hands them to me to dry and put away. It's almost like she's being careful not to accidentally touch me again. That's what I should want, for her to keep her distance, but it's the last thing I want from her.

"Dinner was good tonight," I say to get her talking.

Sky finally gives me a little smile, even if she doesn't meet my eyes.

This time, when I take the pan from her, our fingers touch. That innocent connection has my body reacting in a not-so-innocent way as my heart races and my cock twitches.

I set the pan down on the counter and gently place a hand on her waist. I hope she takes a small step toward me. I don't know what I'm doing, but I want to see where this goes. I'm not stopping it this time.

Neither of us says anything, but her eyes never leave mine as she places her hand on my chest. She used to do that all the time, right before she kissed me. Suddenly all I can see are images of this beautiful, sexy girl kissing me, and before I know it, I'm doing just that.

My mouth lands on her soft lips, and she melts into me like she used to. It's as if no time has passed, and she's still mine. I slowly taste her lips, savoring every detail in case I don't get this chance again. I've learned that you never know when a kiss will be your last.

I wrap my arms around her and pull her body against mine. She has a few more curves since the last time we kissed, but they mold to my body perfectly, and I allow my hands to run over them, getting to know her again.

She pulls back much sooner than I'd have liked and stares into my eyes. She has to know who I am by now, right?

I don't like the idea of her thinking she's kissing someone else. I want her to know it's me. I never planned this, and another chance with her wasn't even in the cards until now. But if we go down that road, I need to be sure she knows who I am. I can't kiss her again or move forward without her knowing.

I place a light kiss on her forehead and take a step back.

"Go get some sleep. I'll see you in the morning," I say, watching her walk out the back door, across the yard, and up the stairs to her apartment.

Only once she's out of sight do I turn and head to my room. I go straight to the bathroom and stare at myself. I haven't done this since I was injured. I know the scar is there, but I don't need to be reminded daily.

I don't see a hint of myself under the long hair and the beard. I have to know she sees me as we move forward. I don't see myself in the mirror, so how can she?

So, I do what I thought I never would. I grab the scissors and say goodbye to Dash.

Chapter 11

SKY

I get up the next morning and get dressed. Nothing fancy, just leggings and a t-shirt to go and make breakfast. I've started taking a shower at midday after I do the cleaning but before I start lunch.

Usually, I'm the first one up, and I've never once thought about my outfit choice until this morning. I walk into the kitchen, and Dash is standing there. His back is to me, looking out the kitchen window.

"Good morning," I say and head to the fridge to get going on breakfast.

He doesn't say anything but turns to look at me. My gasp leaves my mouth before I can stop myself.

There is no mistaking that the man standing in front of me is my ex, Corey. But he's also Dash, the man I've gotten to know in the last few weeks. As he stands in front of me, looking nervous and unsure, my brain tries to combine two people into this man.

In the last few weeks, I've never known Dash to be shy or care what anyone thinks. But the man in front of me is Corey, and I've seen his insecurities. He could never hide them from me.

I *knew* I recognized him. In my heart, I knew it was him. Things felt the same as when I was him, but I never made that connection.

"You did this for me?" I ask, still trying to make sense of everything.

"Yes."

"Why?" I want to know why now, but I can't get the whole thought out.

"I wanted you to see me," he says, still unsure.

I don't know how to act or how I feel. I need some time to figure it out. "I think I'm going to head into town this morning." That is all I say.

"Go. I'll make breakfast," he says in a flat tone.

I nod and head back to my apartment, changing my clothes in a daze. I don't remember getting into my car until I'm driving down the road and almost in town.

Then I started to get pissed. Pissed, he tried to hide who he was. Pissed everyone kept it from me. Who knew this was Corey? Jenna wasn't around before he left, but the church ladies were. Ben? They had to have known.

Did my parents know? My guess is not. They don't run in those circles with any of those people. They would have dismissed him with just a look.

I park in the town square, and the first person I see is Ben. I head straight for him. "Did you know?"

He doesn't ask what I'm talking about, which confirms my suspicions.

He nods toward his police car. "Come sit in here so we have privacy." He opens the passenger door for me. "Yes, I knew, but he asked me not to tell anyone. I'm pretty sure I'm the only one who knew it was him. Besides that, we were friends back in school, so bro code and all." He shrugs. "It wasn't my story to tell."

"That's bullshit and you know it. I had a right to know before taking that job."

"You had no idea after all these weeks?"

I shake my head.

"He isn't the man you knew in high school. Dash has—"

"Corey. His name is Corey," I interrupt.

"No, he's Dash now. The military changed him, and he isn't the same guy. You know it, too. You should get to know him as he is now."

"He shouldn't have hidden it." I cross my arms and sit back in the seat.

Ben studies me. "Did something happen between you two?"

I don't answer.

Ben sighs. "How did you find out?

"He cut his hair and shaved his beard after we kissed last night. I saw it this morning."

"Wow. As a guy myself, I think I have the authority to say that's huge, Sky. What did you say?"

"I asked him why and if he did it for me. Then I left. I was trying to merge Corey and Dash into one person, and I couldn't do it while standing in front of him."

"Talk to him, Sky. He put himself out there, and you walked off."

"Because I didn't know what to do. It's a shock discovering that the guy I was getting to know over the last few weeks is my ex. A man I loved and was ready to start a life with, but who walked out of my life without looking back."

"Loved?" Ben raises an eyebrow.

"I don't know how I feel. I locked those feelings up so long ago."

"I understand. I was there, and I saw what it did to you. My advice is to be honest with him. Take this time to talk and get closure, if nothing else."

"I'll think about it. I'm going for a drive before I head back. I need to think about what I want to say first." I reach over and give him an awkward hug.

As I step out of the car, I spy a few of the ladies from church in the square. "We're going to keep them talking." I nod in their direction.

Ben chuckles. "Let them think what they want. Maybe they'll stop trying to set me up."

"Be careful, pookey! I'll see you tonight. Muah!" I say loudly enough for them to hear.

Ben laughs as I close the door and walk to my car without sparing them a glance. I take the road to circle the lake before heading back to Dash's place.

No matter what, he's still Dash in my head. I think back over the last few weeks. He danced around the subject, but he didn't outright lie to me.

He knew who I was the whole time. Why give me the job? If I hadn't shown up on his doorstep that day, would he have ever talked to me again?

When I get back to the ranch, I find Dash alone in the barn. He turns toward me when he hears me walk in. Neither of us says anything. After an hour's drive, I still have no idea what to say, but I see Corey now, more so than this morning.

He watches me as I slowly approach him. I hesitate for a moment before gently touching the large scar on his face. This man is a grown-up version of my Corey, a sexier version.

"Welcome home, soldier," I whisper and lean in and softly kiss his scar.

He shudders and wraps his arms around my waist, burying his head in my neck.

"Corey—"

"Dash. It's Dash now, sweetheart."

"Dash. Let's take this slow. I'm still trying to process."

He nods and takes a step back. "Have you eaten?"

"No."

He takes my hand, and we head to the house.

"Sit. Let me cook for you." He pulls out a chair at the dining room table.

"But that's my job," I protest.

"And today, it's mine. The ranch hands took sandwiches with them for lunch, so we won't be bothered," he says as he puts together a BLT sandwich I assume he cooked up this morning.

He sets a plate in front of me and sits beside me.

The conversation that follows is wonderful. We touch on what we've done since we saw each other. He tells me about boot camp, his time in the military, and the places he's been. We talk about my school, my job in Dallas, and how much I hated it.

We talk until it's time for me to start dinner. We talk all through dinner and long into the night.

"Let me walk you to your door," he says.

"It's right there. I'll be fine," I tell him.

"If you think I haven't made sure you got to your door okay each night, you don't know me. Now, let me walk you."

He leans in at the top of the stairs and kisses me softly. "Goodnight, sweetheart," he says as I step into my living room.

I think it's safe to say I never got over this man.

Chapter 12

SKY

I get back to my room and reflect on what a great day it's been. Even with the discovery of Dash being Corey, I was just relieved that he was home safe.

I call Sarah because I know she'll come here and kill me herself if I don't tell her something like this.

"Hey, girl. Mac and I were just talking about dates for the lake."

"After what I'm about to tell you, you're probably going to want to do it sooner rather than later."

"Do I need to sit down? I feel like this is something I'm going to need to sit down for," she says, and I can hear some shuffling in the background.

"I would definitely sit down."

"Okay if I put Mac on the phone, too?"

"Yeah. You'd have to tell him anyway," I sigh.

She giggles because it's the truth. "Okay, spill it."

"Dash is Corey."

There's not a word from the other end of the line. She's quiet for so long I pull the phone away from my ear to check it's still connected.

"Corey is the ex-boyfriend, right?" Mac asks.

"Yes," I confirm.

"I've never seen my wife in shock, but I'm pretty sure she's in shock right now." He chuckles, and there's a little squeak on the other end of the phone.

"I think I'm going to need you to explain," Sarah says.

So, I start with my visit to the store and how Dash seemed vaguely familiar, but that the sparks were there when we touched. I tell her I took dinner out to him to try to figure out who he was, how well we got along, and our time getting to know each other on the ranch. I confess about the flirting and kisses and how he cut his hair, and that's when I put two and two together.

And finally, about running into Ben in town and my conversation with Dash through dinner, right up to him walking me to my door.

"Wow. Just... wow," Sarah says.

I know the feeling. "It's hard to combine Dash and Corey as one person, isn't it?"

"Yeah, it is. Have you managed to do it?" she asks.

"I'm working on it, but for the most part, yes."

"Are you going to give him a second chance?"

"I want to see where things go, but there's a strong possibility."

"I want to meet him as he is now." There's some muffled noise and whispers in the background before she starts talking again. "We were looking at making plans for a few weeks from now, but I think we'll come up this weekend."

"I'll talk to him and make sure he's okay with that. If not, we can at least have a girl's night at the lake house."

"Better be up for it; a girl's night is mandatory, no matter what."

"I agree."

"Plus, we're coming to see Jesse and Natalie and their new baby. Ann Mae hasn't stopped talking about that little one, and I'm jealous that I haven't met him yet."

"Sounds like a plan. I haven't met him yet, either. And I haven't run into them in town. It seems they're keeping to themselves right now."

"Can't blame them. Newlyweds and a new baby. I'd hide from the world, too. "

We say our goodbyes, and I get ready for bed. I lie there and figure out how I'm going to approach this subject with Dash.

• • • ● • ● • • •

The next morning, I get up a little earlier, trying to beat Dash into the kitchen before breakfast, but no such luck. He's already there and has the coffee going.

I dressed up a bit today in jeans and a T-shirt, not my usual leggings, and did my hair instead of throwing it up in a messy bun.

"Shoot. I was hoping to beat you up. You've been up before me every morning this week."

Dash offers me a small smile and hands me a cup of coffee.

"Thanks." I take the coffee from him and head to the refrigerator to get my creamer when I realize he's already added it. I take a sip, and the coffee is exactly how I like it. "You've been paying attention."

"Hasn't changed much since high school, just no more sugar," he says, referring to the vanilla creamer I like in my coffee.

"What about your coffee? Still only half and half?"

"Nope. Straight black now. That's all you get on deployment, and you learn to love it."

I sip my coffee and think about my talk with Sarah.

"Out with it," Dash says, startling me from my thoughts.

"What?" I ask, more to buy time than because I didn't hear him.

"I can tell something is on your mind."

"Oh. Well, remember Sarah?"

"Do I remember your best friend? Yes, I remember her." The corners of his eyes crinkle in amusement, and I'm momentarily distracted.

"I talked to her last night." I pause, trying to gather my thoughts.

"I'd be shocked if you didn't."

"She married Mac, and his family has the lake house next to my parents. They're coming up this weekend. Mostly because they want to see Jesse and Natalie's baby. Jesse is Anna Mae's brother, and she married Ella's brother. Ella married Jason, Mac's brother."

"Am I supposed to know any of these people?" he asks with a frown.

"No, I guess not. They all live in Rock Springs."

"Okay, sweetheart. What was the point of all that?"

"Oh, um, Sarah and Mac will be here this weekend, and they want to meet you. Well, Mac wants to meet you. Sarah wants to see you again," I ramble.

"I don't know..." He hesitates.

"It's fine. I'd like to have dinner with them one night if that's okay."

"You should have your friend here if that's what you want. I can stop in and say hi if it's important to you."

"I'd appreciate it."

"Okay. Sounds like a plan."

He pulls me in for a gentle kiss on the forehead, but when we hear the back door opening, we ricochet to opposite sides of the kitchen and act as if nothing happened.

Chapter 13

DASH

Sarah and Mac are arriving today, so I stick close to the house and cut my day shorter so I can say hello for a bit.

Since my time in the military, meeting new people hasn't been easy. They focus on my scar and not on me. So, I've been preparing myself for that all day. Sarah will remember the old me, so I'm expecting the look of pity in her eyes as she mourns the boy I used to be.

Mac didn't know me before, so all he'll see is the scar. It's fifty-fifty if he'll see anything beyond that.

Whatever their reaction, I'll endure it for Sky. This is her best friend, and they were inseparable growing up. I don't have a chance in hell with her if I don't at least make an effort.

A truck I don't recognize is in the drive. I assume it's Mac and Sarah, and I take my time heading into the house. As I get closer, laughter fills the air, and I stop to enjoy it.

How many nights have I walked up to the house and dreaded the quiet? I wished for the house to be filled with life and noise and not to be alone. I have that now with Sky, and I need to enjoy it. I doubt she'll keep this job longer than she needs to figure out her next steps.

I step inside, and all eyes turn to me. Sarah and the man beside her have curious expressions, but Sky looks at me like she used to before I ruined us. Like I hung the moon. A look I don't deserve any more.

"Dash. We were just talking to Mac about you. You know Sarah, and this is her husband, Mac." Sky introduces us.

Mac is tall and tan with almost black hair. Sky told me a bit about him last night. He grew up on a local Native American reservation in Rock Springs and was adopted by his now parents after some pretty bad abuse from his dad. He's the youngest of the siblings, and he and Sarah fell in love when they met in high school. It's nice that their love story has a happily ever after, even if ours didn't.

"Hey, man. Nice to meet you. Sarah has been filling me in on all the things you three used to do and the trouble you got into back in high school," he says, looking me in the eye.

He doesn't mention my scar or seem uncomfortable with it. It's like it isn't even there.

I smile and shake his hand. "She was a bit of a troublemaker even back then."

When he steps back, Sarah pulls me into a hug. "It's good to see you again, Corey. I'm glad you made it home safe and sound," she says before returning to her husband's side.

"It's good to see you again. And it's Dash now, no longer Corey," I correct.

"Oh, Nick sent a care package for you. Mac, will you get it from the truck?" Sarah says.

"Who's Nick?" I ask.

"He's the chef at the local bar and grill in town. His wife is Sarah's sister-in-law. Well, kind of. His wife is a sister to Jason's wife, and Jason is Mac's brother, so..."

"You lost me again. I'll never keep them all straight." I shake my head.

"It's a small-town thing. Sky, why don't you help Mac? He'll sit there and snack on it if you don't watch him," Sarah says, her eyes on me. I know she intends to talk to me alone.

Sky realizes and hesitantly looks at me. I nod to let her know I'll be fine.

Sarah gets down to business the moment Sky is out the door. "Let's cut to the chase. You hurt Sky big time when you left the way you did. She never got over it, and she built walls so high you'd need Thor to smash them down. Don't get her hopes up if you don't plan on sticking around."

"I know I hurt her. I'm not going anywhere, but I don't think she's staying here. Her dreams are too big for this town. I don't have rose-colored glasses this time. I enjoy being around her, and I want to know who she is now, but most of all, I want to give her the closure she needs. I owe her that."

Sarah stares at me for a moment before she nods. "Just don't hurt her again."

I don't get a chance to answer because Sky and Mac walk in with a box full of food.

"Jenna just called. She's on her way over," Sky says as we head to the kitchen. She unloads the box and shares a few samples of food with us. Whoever this Nick guy is, he sure can cook.

We eat some and talk. It's good to talk with people about something other than work.

"Did Sarah tell you she was always my alibi?" Sky asks with a laugh.

"I can see that." Mac nods.

"Once, Dash and I were watching a movie at Sarah's when her parents were out of town."

"My parents always had a nanny to watch me and were rarely home. The nanny was happy to have us there so she could watch us rather than us sneaking around," Sarah adds.

"Well, my mom called because I wasn't home and it was an hour past curfew. Sarah convinced my mom we had sleepover plans she'd agreed to and forgotten. The nanny covered for us and everything," Sky says with a laugh.

"If I remember correctly, you two were cleaning toilets and polishing silverware the next day as punishment," I add.

"Oh, yeah. We paid the price for that one, but nothing as bad as my parents finding out," Sky says.

There's a hesitant knock on the door. Sky moves to answer it, and I stop her.

"It's just Jenna," she says.

"It probably is, but let me answer, just in case."

She nods and stays back with her friends. I don't grab the shotgun because I don't want to scare Jenna off, but it's in range if the person on the other side isn't Jenna.

"Hi Dash, I'm Jenna." She extends her hand, and I shake it.

Just like Mac and Sarah, she looks at me, not my scar.

"They're waiting on you in the kitchen. Come on in," I tell her, and she follows me into the house.

"Jenna!" Sarah greets her with a huge hug.

"Okay. Us girls are going to my apartment to chat. You men have fun!" Sky says, pulling them out the door.

"Have fun, and remember, only fifty percent of what she says about me is true!" Mac calls after them.

"You want a beer?" I ask him after the girls have gone.

He smiles. "Yeah, maybe a tour of your setup, too. I could use a good walk."

I laugh. "That's what makes your family the second biggest ranch in the state of Texas."

"And tied   for second largest in the country!"

We walk outside toward the barn.

"My dad taught me the same thing. Always check out what other ranches are doing, no matter their size. You never know what you can learn," I tell him.

An hour later, over a beer on the back porch, I realize I haven't hung out with someone like this since my days at my first duty station.

It's nice to shoot the shit, even if he's only here for Sky.

· · · ● ●· ● ● · · ·

Sky

"You know, back home, we have these girls' nights once a month with everyone. We catch up and have some good food, maybe some drinks. I love it," Sarah says.

"It's been so long since I've had a girls' night like this," I tell her.

"That makes two of us. We should make this the start of our girls' nights. We can get Austin, Natalie, and Candy to join, I bet," Jenna says.

"I'd like that. But I'm not sure how long I'll be here," I say.

They both turn to look at me.

"This was temporary. I was supposed to find out what I was doing next before my parents figured it out. I'm shocked they haven't already."

"Honestly, me too. Everyone is talking about it," Jenna agrees.

"Great," I grumble. I turn to Sarah to change the subject. "What's going on In Rock Springs?"

"Megan is pregnant again. Lilly is pregnant, too, and so is her horse, Black Diamond. Kelly seemed to fall off the face of the Earth, so things have been pretty boring otherwise."

"What about you, Jenna? I know your brothers are on the hunt for a ranch. How are they doing on it?" I ask.

"They're still saving but have started looking. They say they'll know the right place when they find it."

Jenna has three older brothers, and they have this dream of owning and running a ranch together.

"Okay, we've talked about everything we can. Now you have to talk about Dash," Sarah says.

"I don't know what to say. I keep seeing the boy I was in love with all those years ago. The one I'd have waited for if he had only asked. But he's different. I want to get to know this new side of him."

"I think that's why you haven't done your research on what you want to do next. I don't think you want to leave," Jenna says.

"I agree. I think there was something there even before you knew it was Corey. It's why you took this job," Sarah says.

I can't deny it because there is something there, and I wanted to figure it out. The job to save me from my parents was just a bonus, though now I can see why he offered it.

"Yeah, but I can't let it be the reason I stay."

Chapter 14

Dash

Yesterday went well. Mac and Sarah are good people, and it's great to see Sarah so happy and that Mac treats her well. Jenna is a great addition to Sky's friends. The three of them get along so well. It's great to see Sky smile and be as happy as she is around them.

Seeing Mac and Sarah together made me realize that could have been us if I hadn't walked away. If I had let her wait for me like she wanted, I know that would be us right now.

I wouldn't have woken up in that hospital alone. I would have had her by my side the whole time. I could kick my ass for what I did to us.

But now I have what feels like a second chance, and I'm not going to waste it.

I'm up again before Sky and I get the coffee going. Like every morning lately, we cook breakfast and eat together. But before I head to the barn, I want to ask her a question.

"So, I was thinking. Would you like to have dinner with me at the diner later this week?" I ask before I lose my courage.

She smiles. "Yeah, I'd like that. But maybe later today, you can make time to go for a ride with me? The weather has been so nice, and I'd love to take advantage of it."

We used to ride together every weekend, which was a great way to spend time together.

"Yeah, I'd like that. Let's take lunch out, yeah?" I already have a few ideas running through my head.

"Yeah, I'd like that. See you then," she says as I head out the door.

My mind is on Sky all morning, and the ranch hands have to go behind me and fix my mistakes.

"Hey, man. Hell, if I can tell you what to do, but I think maybe you should give up on working today. We can get more done without you here," Drake says.

"Fuck. I'm sorry, man. My head is somewhere else today."

"It's okay. You head off. We got this, boss."

I head to my room to clean up. Sky and I used to go riding all the time, so I don't know why I'm so nervous. Once ready, I go downstairs and find Sky setting lunch out for the guys.

"I figure we could take ours to go." She holds up a picnic basket.

"Perfect. I know just the spot."

We saddle up the horses and head out on a trail I haven't ridden in a while. Mostly because I don't get to ride for fun anymore, but also because it's full of memories of Sky.

"I love this part of the ranch," she says, taking off at a gallop.

I let her lead because she looks so carefree and full of life. Before I know it, we're at the field where we had picnics, and she's setting up a blanket under our tree.

"This tree has grown even bigger. I didn't think that was possible," she says, walking around it and staring up at the branches.

I get my horse settled and join her. "I haven't been back here since I've been home."

Sky looks at me. "Why not?"

I shrug, not wanting to talk about the truth yet. "I haven't had time."

"I'm glad because I like that our first time back here is together."

All our firsts happened under this tree. The first time we kissed when I asked her to be my girlfriend. Our first dance, our first make-out session, and when I asked her to prom. We even lost our virginity to each other under this tree.

"Yeah, I think you're right." I hold my hand out to her, and she takes it. Those same sparks are still there, and I wonder if they will ever go away. Will I ever not feel like a teenager around her?

I lead Sky to the blanket and the basket of food. She pulls out some sandwiches, chips, cookies, and water. Nothing fancy, but then again, the last time we had a picnic here, we'd just turned eighteen, so neither of us was drinking.

We chat about Sarah, Mac, and Jenna visiting yesterday and share our favorite memories under this tree. The conversation is lighthearted until we finish lunch. We haven't talked about the best memories here, the kisses, touches, and the sex.

But they're at the front of my mind, and I'm sure they're on her mind as well.

As she talks, I can't help but watch her lips and wonder if they taste the same as the last time we were here. They pull me in without my knowledge because I'm closer than I realized when she lets out a little gasp and then leans into me.

Our lips meet, and I swear I hear angels singing behind us. It's a perfect moment. The girl I've thought about so much and was my sole focus on my deployments. The one I will never forget is here with me in one of our favorite spots.

I would never have thought that possible a year ago, or hell, even six months ago.

I cup the back of her neck and hold her to me as I slowly lay her down on the blanket. I never break the contact between my lips and hers.

"You still taste the same," I whisper against her lips.

She smiles and continues to kiss me as I brace myself over her. Her body still fit against mine like she was made for me.

"I always loved it when you caged me in like this," she says.

I pull back enough to frame her face with my hands and lock my gaze with hers.

"I'll make it a point to do it more often." I smile before leaning in to kiss her again.

I taste her like this might be the last time I get the chance. I didn't know the last time I kissed her would be the last all those years ago, so I plan to cherish each kiss I get now.

Her lips are soft and taste like the vanilla ChapStick she always uses. She wraps her arms around my neck, running her hands through my hair and knocking my hat off.

Just having her hands on me makes me hard, and there's no way to hide my length digging into her leg.

When she rubs against it, I moan because it feels so good, and I want to relieve it more than anything. But I'm not letting us go there just yet. I don't want to move that fast.

So, I pull back and place a soft kiss on her forehead before sitting up. "We have plenty of time, sweetheart. Let's not rush it."

Sky snuggles into my side and rests her head on my shoulder as we stare across the field like we've done so many times before.

Chapter 15

SKY

I have a date.

It's been well over a year since I've been on a date, and that one was to make my parents happy. I didn't want to be there, and I was nowhere near as nervous as I am now for my date with Dash.

Not just any date, though. This is our date at the diner. It's not a fancy place, but I know exactly what it means. It will put us out there for everyone to see. The whole town will be talking about it, which means my parents will find out. It also means that the man who has kept himself locked away on his ranch is willing to push himself out of his comfort zone to go someplace he knows I like.

I know Jenna is working tonight, and I hope having a familiar face there will make him a little more comfortable. Jenna told Austin we'll be there, so I'm sure Austin will be there too. And if

I know Walker Lake like I think I do, before we finish our meal, half the town will be in the diner to see Dash.

There's a knock on my door, and I smile. Ever the gentleman, picking me up for a date. I open the door, and my mouth goes dry. Dash looks so handsome in dark jeans, a button-down shirt, a cowboy hat, and boots. This man looks like sin walking, and I am here for whatever ride he's willing to take me on.

"You look beautiful," he says, running his eyes over me.

"You clean up pretty well yourself, cowboy." I finally meet his eyes and smile.

He takes my hand and leads me down the stairs and across the front yard to his truck, where he opens the door and helps me inside. He waits until I've buckled up before closing the door and making his way over to his side of the truck.

Just like that, it's like no time has passed between us. He drives, I control the radio, and the conversation is easy and fun. It isn't until we park his truck in the town square that reality sinks in.

"We can grab some food to go and eat by the lake, just the two of us," I suggest, offering him an out.

"You deserve so much better than that. I can handle this." He smiles and takes a deep breath before stepping out of the truck.

He opens my door, holding his hand out for me to take and helping me down. He doesn't drop my hand as we head inside. Almost like it's been choreographed, all eyes shift to us as we step inside, and the diner goes deadly quiet.

I smile and nod at everybody as if they aren't gawking at who I'm here with. This seems to snap them out of whatever trance they're in, and they go back to their conversations and food.

Dash takes the side of the booth facing the rest of the diner and allows me to sit with my back to everyone.

"If you want to change spots so you don't have to look at them staring at you, I'm more than happy to," I offer.

"Thanks, but I prefer not to have my back to the door."

Jenna comes over and brings us some menus. "Hey, Sky. Good to see you again, Dash. What can I get you two to drink?" she asks as if it's an everyday thing for us to walk into the diner together and grab a meal.

Hopefully, everyone will take her lead and not make a big deal. We place our drink orders, and Jenna heads off.

The conversation isn't as easy as it was in the truck. I can tell Dash is uncomfortable, and while he's focused on me, every so often, he glances around the diner.

"Hey, ignore them. This is the first time they've seen us together. The more they see you out, the less they will care," I tell him.

Dash offers me a strained smile.

"Hey, Sky. Jenna sent me over," Austin greets as she walks up to the table.

"Dash, this is Austin. She runs the place. Her aunt owns the diner." I introduce them.

"It's nice to officially meet you. I took over about two years ago. I've been trying to get to know everyone in town," she says to Dash.

After that, the rest of the dinner seems to go pretty easily. A few people stop to say hi, but otherwise, they leave us alone. We finish our meal, and Dash doesn't let me get my wallet out of my purse.

"Don't even think about it, Sky. This is a date, and I'm paying. Don't insult me by trying to pay."

I chuckle and let him do his thing. "Do you want to walk down to the lake?"

The lake is only a few blocks from the town square. It's well-lit and a beautiful walk at night.

"Let's do it." He takes my hand and leads the way.

Once we reach the lake, Dash steps behind me and wraps his arms around my waist. A simple moment, but it feels so intimate. I'm still turned on from our time in the field yesterday, and this only adds to it.

We stand there for a little while in silence, watching the reflection of the moon dance on the lake before Dash leans down and whispers in my ear, "You ready to head home?" His grip on my waist tightens, pulling me against him so I can feel his hardness.

I'm hoping he means something more than just dropping me off at my door. I turn around in his arms to face him. "Let's go."

The whole drive home, his hand is on my thigh, and the tension in the truck is palpable. He glances over at me every so often, and the heat in his eyes sets off butterflies in my stomach.

"Would you like to come inside?" I ask before we get out of the truck, hoping I haven't misread this whole night.

"Oh, I definitely plan on coming inside you tonight, sweetheart," he says before his lips land on mine.

When he pulls back, he leads me into the house and slams the door behind us.

Dash

"If this isn't what you want, you better stop me now," I warn Sky as I take a step toward her.

She takes a step back until she hits the wall. "I want this," she whispers.

That's all I need. I remove my boots and belt with my eyes still locked on her. Sky removes her shoes and sets her purse down.

"If you don't want to do this here, you know where my room is. I suggest you get there now," I growl because my room is the one place I haven't had her. I was never brave enough to try it.

"Maybe I want you to fuck me right here against the wall," she says with a flirty smile.

"I hope you mean it because that is exactly what you're going to get." I wrap one arm around her waist and place the other on the wall beside her head.

I lean in for a kiss as she wraps her hands around my neck. I pull back enough to remove her shirt and bra along with my shirt.

Her nipples are hard, showing she's as turned on as I am. My cock is straining against my jeans, wanting to be inside her.

I cup each of her breasts. They're a bit larger than the last time we were together. Running my thumbs over her nipples, she moans and throws her head back against the wall, pushing her chest into my hands.

"You are so damn beautiful," I tell her, at a loss for a word to describe this woman in front of me.

I bend and suck one nipple into my mouth while cupping her core over her jeans. Just feeling her heat sends me into a frenzy, needing to be skin-to-skin. I quickly remove her pants and mine. Her underwear and my boxers hit the floor shortly after, but not before pulling the condom from my wallet I put there after our time in the field yesterday.

I slide the condom on before pinning her back to the wall again. She wraps her arms around my neck before giving a cute little jump and wrapping her legs around my waist, pressing her warm, wet pussy to my cock.

I groan, pinning her to the wall and reaching between us to position my cock.

"You are mine, Sky. You have always been mine." I don't realize I've said that out loud until she replies.

"Just like you have always been mine."

No truer words have been spoken. She held my heart, body, and soul from the first moment I saw her all those years ago. I will always belong to her, and I know that with absolute certainty.

As I slide inside her, a feeling of completeness fills me. This is home, and this is what I have been missing.

She moans as I fill her and digs her heels into my ass. "Fuck, I forgot how good you feel," she gasps, gripping my hair.

"I never forgot one second with you, sweetheart."

I start at a slow, steady pace that does exactly what I want—drives her crazy. She tries to increase the pace, but I don't allow her to take control.

I run my hands over every inch of her I can reach and allow myself to enjoy being inside her. This is a moment I thought I'd never get to experience again.

When she lets out a frustrated groan, I smile. I follow with a groan when she clamps her walls around me.

"Fuck," I hiss.

"Not so fun when you're the one being teased, huh?" she asks, doing it again.

Leave it to this girl to find a way to be sassy even when she's stuffed full of my cock. I finally relent and give her what we both need—a race to the finish.

I angle my hips to hit her clit with each thrust. Thankfully, I live alone because anyone in this house would hear me pounding her into the wall.

"Fuck. Fuck. Fuuuuckkkkk..." Sky moans before she comes all over my cock in the most beautiful moment I can ever recall.

I try to watch, but I follow her over the edge, and it's all I can do to keep us from falling to the ground with the intensity of the orgasm that hits me.

This girl has ruined me, and she doesn't even know it.

Chapter 16

DASH

I've always been an early riser. It's something that's drilled into you when you live on a ranch and even more so in the military. Even when I try to sleep in, I can't, especially when a girl as beautiful as Sky is beside me.

I make breakfast for the ranch hands and let her sleep in. I'm about to take her breakfast in bed when there's a knock on the door.

Answering it, I find Ben on the other side.

"Sorry to show up unannounced, but I wanted to let you know we've had more issues with the land developer. They cut the fences on a couple of ranches to get equipment in the fields. We aren't sure what they were doing, but it would probably be a good idea to have your guys ride the fence line to make sure everything's still intact."

"Hopefully, they aren't stupid enough that they've done that here. I already told them the next time I saw them I'd shoot first and ask questions later."

"That's what we've been informing all the ranchers to do since they're not taking no for an answer. My boss went over there and let them know that per Texas law, there's nothing we can do, so the landowners they were trespassing on started shooting at them. Knowing him, he probably told them we were advising them to do so. We're hoping that stops them and scares them out of town."

"We can only hope. Thank you for the heads up."

"You're welcome. Have you and Sky talked after she found out who you are?"

I'm confused about how he knew that, and he must have been able to read it on my face.

"I ran into her in town the day she found out. She was pissed at me because I didn't tell her." He answers the question I didn't ask.

"Yeah, we've been talking and went on a date last night. I'm surprised you haven't heard about it. I'm sure everyone in town stopped at the diner to see for themselves while we were there." I shake my head.

"The diner was my next stop to grab some coffee. I'm sure I'll hear about it then. Can I ask why you waited so long to tell her?"

"Honestly, I was scared and wanted some time with her. I fully expected her to walk away when she found out who I was. She had no reason to give me a second chance, and I never expected her to."

"I get that. Just a heads up, I didn't know about the date, but I think her parents have heard. The guy I work with, his parents are friends with Sky's parents, and he told me they're pissed off about who she's been hanging out with lately. I'm assuming that means you."

"Yeah, it probably is. Are the land developers still focused on the Silver Cattle Ranch?" I ask, trying to get off the subject of Sky.

"Yes, but he's holding out and not selling to them. The longer they go without getting property here, the more desperate they're getting. I'm not sure why they aren't moving on."

"Well, if you need anything, let me know. I'm happy to help and get these guys to move on as soon as possible."

Ben's eyes dart behind me, and I turn to see Sky stepping into the room wearing my shirt and her hair a mess. There's no hiding what happened last night.

"That's my cue. I'll leave you be. Call me if you hear more about the developers," Ben says before leaving me alone with Sky.

"Get your butt back in that bed," I tell her, confident that neither one of us will be getting anything done today.

Chapter 17

SKY

It's been a few days since our date at the diner. We haven't left the ranch and are enjoying some time together. We're having breakfast when my phone pings with a text message. My gut tells me I don't want to know who it is, but I check out of duty.

Mom: Dinner tonight. We know you're still in town.

"Everything okay?" Dash asks.

"My parents have summoned me. My guess is they heard about us." I don't answer my mom. She's not expecting me to.

"You going?"

"I figure I should. The longer I put it off, the worse it will be."

"Do you want me to go with you?" he asks.

I can tell it's the last thing he wants to do, and I don't blame him. "No, it's probably better that you don't. I'll go see what they know and decide from there what I want to do."

"Okay. Will you call me if you need anything? I'll probably head into town tonight, so I'll be close if you need me," he says.

I know how he works. "By heading to town, you mean you're going to sit at the park down the road from my parents' house, right?" I ask with a smile.

He doesn't answer. He just gives me a look that says, you know exactly what I mean.

The rest of the day flies by, and when I step outside to get ready to head to my parents, Dash is there, ready to go.

"I'll follow you into town, and if you need anything just call," he says, opening my car door.

"I'll be fine. Maybe go to the diner and grab some dinner. That way, you're not sitting in your car wasting away to nothing." I doubt he'll take my advice, but I hope he will.

As promised, he follows me into town and along the road that takes me around the lake to my parents' house. He pulls into the park, and I keep going. There's something comforting about knowing he's close by, just in case.

I pull into the driveway and look at my parents' house. It's beautiful, with a stone facade. Growing up, this house seemed so small, like it was trapping me here. Now, knowing what's waiting on the other side of the door, it feels huge and scary.

I take a deep breath. I need to get this over with. I knock on the front door because I know it will irritate my mom to get up and answer it, only to find me on the other side.

"Hi, Mom," I say when the door opens.

The bright smile on my mom's face falls. "Why are you knocking?" she huffs as she walks off.

"Because I don't live here, and it's the polite thing to do," I say, knowing she doesn't really want an answer.

I set my purse on the table by the door but tuck my phone into my pocket. I followed my mom to the back of the house toward the big living area overlooking the lake.

"Dinner will be ready in about ten minutes. Let's sit and chat about this job of yours," my mom says as she joins my dad on the couch.

I sit across from them in one of the oversized leather chairs.

"What about it?" I ask, thinking she means my job at the ranch.

"What's going on with your job in Dallas?" my dad asks, straight to the point.

"I don't have a job in Dallas. The company was going under, and they kept piling on more work while cutting my pay."

"So, you up and left without a backup plan?" he asks, but I know it's a rhetorical question.

"I've been putting in resumes all over town, but my boss found out about it and started blocking them so I couldn't get another job. I wasn't happy in Dallas, so it was a sign to get out of there. The rent was about to go up on my apartment, so I didn't renew. I packed up my stuff and put it in storage."

"And now, what's your plan? You have some menial job at a ranch?" my mom demands.

"I plan to figure out my next steps and not rush into anything. The job at the ranch is temporary. It's enough to cover my bills and gives me a place to live, so I don't have to touch my emergency savings while I figure it out," I explain, appealing to my parents' practical side.

"Why don't you stop lying to us?" my mother says as a timer goes off in the kitchen.

"We'll finish this over dinner. The least we can do is make sure you're eating properly," my dad says, putting an effective pause on the conversation.

My mom pulls the pans of food from the oven. It's all pre-made, so all she had to do was warm it up.

Once we're sitting down again, my mom looks at me. "We know you were out on a date with The Beast."

"First, his name is Dash. That nickname is bullshit. He's one of the best guys I've ever met, so when he asked me to dinner, I said yes." I wonder if my parents knew that Dash was Corey. I don't have to wonder for long.

"It's like that boy you dated in high school. You don't need a rancher. You need a businessman who'll take care of you, and you're not going to find that here," my mom says.

So, they don't know that Cory and Dash are the same person. That doesn't surprise me because they turn their nose up at the ranchers in town. They're so focused on the people with money and associating with the higher class that it makes me wonder why they live here.

"Well, it's up to me, and Dash has been nothing but generous, giving me a place to stay and a job when I needed it. And he's a good man, despite what people in town might have others believe."

"Then we should meet him properly," my father says.

Shock crosses my mother's face, but he holds his hand up, letting her know he's got this.

"If he's someone you're working for and spending time with, we should get to know him properly. If nothing else, then for your safety."

When my dad puts it like that, it's hard to come up with an excuse to say no.

Can I convince Dash to have dinner with my parents? It will be one hell of dinner because there'll be no hiding who he is when he gets here.

Chapter 18

DASH

Sky: I'm leaving now.

The text comes in, and her car passes the park a few minutes later. I pull up behind her and follow her home. There's no hint of how the dinner went, and I'm interested to find out.

Once home, Sky gets out of the car and heads into the house without waiting for me. When I walk inside after her, she pours herself a glass of whiskey and then hands me one.

"That bad?" I ask.

She glares at me. "They asked what happened to my job in Dallas. Were upset that I didn't have another one lined up, even though my boss sabotaged any interview I tried to take. They don't know who you are, but because we had dinner at the diner and I'm working for you, they would like to meet and have dinner with you."

Of course, they would. Part of me wondered if this would be the outcome of this meal. They want to meet me, not out of curiosity about who I am, but to know how they can spin me to make themselves look good.

"Do you want me to go?" I ask hesitantly. I never got along with her parents, and I don't see that changing anytime soon.

"It would probably be best to get it out of the way. But they don't know who you are. They knew you as The Beast, and I corrected them to Dash. So, it could be a shit show when we get there. I have no idea." Sky chugs down the rest of her whiskey.

I know exactly how this will go down. They won't be thrilled to see me in any capacity. There will be no more hiding. I know her parents will find out the truth when they realize who I am. Maybe that will be enough to push Sky to figure out what she wants.

That's probably for the best.

"When do they want to meet me?" I ask, tossing back the rest of my whiskey and enjoying the burn.

"Tomorrow."

That means I may only have tonight with her. I plan to take full advantage of it. I walk over to her, my eyes never leaving hers. She backs up against the wall, and I pin her there.

"Go get on my bed. We have a long night ahead of us, sweetheart."

If I'm going to lose her, I want one last night to remember.

· · · • · • · · ·

I step out of the car and take a deep breath. Sky's parents' home is beautiful, but it always looked a bit like a prison to me, without the bars on the windows.

"The sooner we get this over with, the sooner we can go home and forget this night ever happened," Sky says, holding her hand out to me.

I think we have very different ideas about how this night will end. I want it to go her way, but I know it won't.

She rings the doorbell, and her mom opens the door with a fake smile. It's clear to see the moment she recognizes me.

"What's he doing here?" she demands.

"Mom, this is Dash."

"No, that's Corey," she says, dropping the smile altogether.

"He goes by Dash now," Sky says.

Her mom moves aside, and Sky pulls me into the house. If looks could kill, the one her mom is giving me would put me six feet under.

I walk into the living room, and her dad stands to greet us. When he sees me, he looks at Sky. "I thought we were meeting Dash, the man you're working for," he says, his distaste evident.

"This is who I'm working for. He goes by Dash now."

"I thought we were rid of you when we made you join the military." Sky's dad doesn't even try to hide what happened with his daughter standing right here.

"What do you mean, made him join the military?" she asks, dropping my hand and looking between the two of us.

"He was never good enough for you, so we persuaded him to make the right choice. Join the military, get his school paid for that way, and leave you alone," her dad says.

Sky looks at me dumbstruck. "Is that what happened?" Her voice is soft in a way I don't deserve.

"I was young and easily manipulated, but yes. He made it seem like I had no other choice. At the end of his talk, I was convinced you wouldn't wait for me. But in the end, it was the choice I made that broke us, so that's on me." I tell her honestly.

I've had so long to think about this and us. It took a few years to realize I was manipulated, but it was my decision. Maybe I wasn't strong enough to disobey her parents. Maybe it was that I thought Sky was too good for me. Whatever the reason, it wasn't hard for her father to get in my head and convince me I was a lost cause.

"That's bullshit. I would have waited for you. I know that now, and I knew it then. You had other options." She turns to face her father. "You knew he had other options. You did what was in your best interests because I wasn't following the path *you* wanted. You didn't give a damn about what *I* wanted." Her voice rises with each word.

"He can't leave this town because of that ranch. He was born on that ranch, and he will die on that ranch. It doesn't matter that he got out of town for a little while. You, on the other hand, can have a life far beyond this little town," her mom says.

"But the same town is good enough for the two of you?" Sky demands.

"We have our reasons for being here, and they are none of your concern," her father says.

"Newsflash! I hated my life in Dallas. I hated the seventy-hour work weeks. I hated how loud it was. I hated how busy it was. I hated how I was a stranger, even in my apartment building. I love it here. I love walking into the diner and knowing the people there. I love that the waitress knows my order. I love how quiet and slow-paced it is. You don't get to choose my life!"

I'm proud of Sky for sticking up for herself. I know she's always wanted to make her parents proud, but she wanted to do it on her terms.

"As for you"—she spins to face me—"*I* get to decide my life. You had no right to make that choice for me. I would like to go home now."

She turns and stomps to the front door without another word. I look at the two people I've been dreading facing for years, *really* look at them. The stress they live their lives under has aged them. They were so scary to me as a teenager. Now, I could not care less.

I turn and follow Sky without a word.

Chapter 19

SKY

"Will you tell me what's going on in that pretty head of yours?" Dash asks after we've left town without a single word between us.

"I don't know who to be madder at. My parents for convincing you to go or for you for listening to them."

"I don't know what you want me to say. Nothing I say now will change the choices I made back then," he says, his voice calm and almost emotionless. I wonder if that's something the military drilled into him.

"I think we should cool things down between us," I tell him as we pull into the ranch.

"Listen, you can be mad all you want. Is what your parents did wrong? Absolutely. But we can't change that now, and I'm not giving up on us."

I shake my head and get out of the car, heading up the stairs to my apartment.

"Your parents were right about one thing. I did join to go to school. I also joined to travel. I needed to see something outside this town," Dash says from the bottom of the steps.

I turn to face him. "That's fine, but I would have waited for you."

"I didn't want you to wait for years, not knowing when we could be together with you going to school and me constantly being deployed. Your parents wouldn't have let you put your whole life on hold like that."

"So you let my parents play on both our insecurities. Once I found out you joined, they were in my ear about how horrible life as a military wife was, yet I wanted it so badly with you."

When Dash doesn't say anything, I head inside, closing the door behind me. I stand there for a few minutes, waiting to see if he goes inside. I don't hear anything, but he's gone when I peek out the window.

I go straight to my room and lie on the bed, trying to make sense of what happened tonight. But my mind keeps straying to Dash. What is he doing? What is he thinking about?

He said he wasn't going to give up on us. My mind focuses on that, and it just goes around and around in my head.

I pull out my phone and call Sarah.

"Hey, girl. How are things going?" she greets me with the sunny personality I love so much.

I don't waste time. I dive in and tell her what's happened in the last few days. We talk for a few hours, and I have a solid game plan by the time we finish our call. Now all I have to do is put it in place.

· · · • · • · • · · ·

Dash

I've been awake all night, and now I lie here waiting for dawn so I can get up. I thought about last night over and over again, every word that was said.

I've decided I want to talk to Sky. I want to fight for her. I screwed things up once, but I'm not doing it again. This time, I'm going to fight for her. I'm going to fight for us.

I make coffee and wait for her to join me, but she doesn't. I make breakfast for the ranch hands before going to check on her.

I knock on her door, but nothing. I knock again and listen. There's no movement inside. Then I notice her car isn't in the driveway. I head back to the house and grab the keys to unlock her door.

The place smells like her, with a few key differences. Her clothes aren't in the closet. Her dresser drawers are open and empty. When I finally make it back to the kitchen, I find a note on the island.

Dash,

Like I said in the car last night, I need space to think and process all of this, and I can't do that here with you.

I'm heading down to spend some time with Sarah in Rock Springs to clear my mind.

I don't know when I'll be back, but I plan to spend my time doing what I should have been doing here—figuring out my next steps.

Sky

She left.

Did she leave last night? It wasn't before I got up this morning. Instead of sticking around to work it out, she left. The worst part is I can't even get mad at her because last time, I was the one who left instead of staying around to talk it out.

It's the perfect taste of my own medicine, isn't it?

But I have to know she's okay. I need to know she made it to Rock Springs safely, if nothing else.

Me: I got your note. Please let me know you're okay.

I didn't expect a text message back so soon.

Sky: I'm fine.

Two words. I guess I deserve that.

Me: Can we talk? Please.

Sky: There's nothing to talk about.

When I get her text, I feel like I can't breathe. I can't lose her again.

How many nights did I stay up in my bunk, thinking of her and promising myself that if I ever got another chance with her, I wouldn't screw it up?

Well, here I am with another chance, and I screwed it up, but I'm sure as hell not letting her go so easily.

Chapter 20

SKY

I arrived in Rock Springs late last night and barely got any sleep. I was up at dawn, lying in bed, when Dash's texts came in.

After that, I knew there was no way I was going back to sleep, so I got up, got dressed, and went for a walk on the ranch. Every ranch looks different at the first light of dawn before people get moving and the ranch comes to life.

If I listen hard enough, I can hear everyone starting their day back at the house, but the further I walk into the field, the quieter it gets. That quiet is what I crave right now. And I know one place on the ranch I'll be sure to get it.

I follow the trail. I've only been out this way a few times, and I've always had Sarah or someone else with me to guide the way, so I pray I'm going the correct way. I pay attention to the trail and landmarks, and before I know it, the little country church pops up from the tree line.

They call it the ranch church, and while it's kept up beautifully, they no longer use it every week. The church started here on the ranch generations ago and is now used primarily for weddings and occasional funerals.

I step inside, expecting to have the place to myself. I'm shocked to see someone sitting at the front, her long, dark brown hair falling down her back.

Megan turns around and greets me with a smile. She's Mac's sister. She owns the beauty salon in town, and her husband is the town vet.

"I'm sorry. I didn't think anyone else would be here," I tell her.

"It's okay. I felt like I should be here today. I told my husband that I was pregnant in that pew right over there. We also did some very un-church-like things there." She laughs, and even from here, I can see her cheeks are bright red.

"Well, it wouldn't be a good church if there weren't some hanky panky in the back pews," I joke.

"I can go and let you have the place to yourself," she says as she stands.

"No need for that. I was just out enjoying the ranch, letting my thoughts get the best of me," I tell her as I sit next to her.

"I've been there. I get the feeling you're here because of a guy. If you don't want to talk, it's okay. But Sarah has already called a girls' night tonight. There will be tacos and margaritas, and you can talk about it and get our opinions or not. Either way, it's the best therapy you can ask for."

Megan pats me on the shoulder, stands, and walks out. After the last few days, I could use some therapy.

• • • ● ●• ● ● • • •

Later that night, we're all gathered in the main house. By all, I mean Sarah's sisters-in-law, her friends, and loosely related family, including Mac's mom and Megan's mother-in-law. All in all, there are about fifteen of us, lots of different tacos, plenty of margaritas, and for dessert, margarita cupcakes. These ladies sure know how to do girls' night.

Once everyone has food and drinks, we take our place in the main living room, where plenty of chairs have been brought in. There's a massive couch and several beanbags on the floor, and everyone is squished together.

I eat as I listen to the town gossip, trying to remember who's who and put faces to names.

"You know Mrs. Willow went out to Vegas again this year. She was in the beauty shop yesterday telling us about her trip. She only told us a little and said certain things must remain in Vegas," Megan says.

"Mrs. Willow is Anna Mae and Jesse's grandma," Sara whispers.

"Did she try to tell you the story of how she could have become some man's sugar baby but turned him down because that's not her thing?" Anna Mae asks.

"Yes!" Megan laughs.

"She tells me that story every time she goes to Vegas. I don't believe it, especially since she went with her new husband this time." Anna Mae laughs.

The conversation continues for a while longer, and I decide to get their opinion in one of the lulls.

I jump in and tell them the story of Dash and Corey. Our date at the diner, my dinner with my parents, and finally, what I found out from the last dinner with my parents, all the way until I ended up here.

"I think the people you should be upset with are your parents. At that age, it's so easy to be manipulated, and your parents took advantage of that," Lilly says. She's a friend of the family.

"I think we already know the answer to this question. We could hear it in the way you talked about him, but maybe you haven't admitted it to yourself. How do you feel about Dash? Is he worth fighting for?" Sage asks.

She's right. I've been so focused on "how dare they do this to me?" that I never stopped to think. I never stopped to realize that I never fell out of love with Dash. To this day, I am still in love with him.

"You should talk to your parents, but you've got to fight for him, sweetheart," Mac's mom says. I've always liked her. She is great for advice but is also willing to step back and let you make your own mistakes, which I know probably isn't easy for a mother.

The rest of the girls' night is a blur as I think and make plans. I'm not letting someone else decide my future this time. I'm not going to let someone else manipulate those around me to get what they want.

No, this time, I'm going to get what I want.

Chapter 21

Dash

I spend the next few days trying to go about my day as if nothing has happened. I'm pretty sure all the ranch hands are scared of me and are giving me a wide berth.

I've been doing anything and everything to keep my mind off Sky. I work from sun up until sundown and sometimes beyond. I organize things that don't need to be organized, clean things that don't need to be cleaned, and ride fences I know are perfectly fine, but none of it helps.

I didn't fight for Sky last time. But it's not too late to go after her. It can't be. I never thought I was good enough for her, but she thinks I am, and that's enough, so long as she still wants me. I will fight for us. I won't let her down again.

I step into the house, unsure of my next move. I know she's in Rock Springs with Sarah, and when Mac was here, we exchanged phone numbers. So I decide to reach out to him.

"Hello," He answers the phone with no emotion in his voice.

"I know that Sky's there, and I know I screwed up, but I need to make this right. I want to come down and do this in person," I tell him honestly.

It's quiet on the other end of the phone for so long that I look to make sure the phone hasn't been disconnected or Mac hasn't hung up on me.

"My wife will probably kill me, but I want nothing more than to see Sky happy. She's done so much for my wife over the years and was there for her when I couldn't be. She's on her way back to Walker Lake now to talk to her parents. She should be there within the next couple of hours, depending on how many stops she makes."

"Thank you. I promise I'm going to make this right."

"I hope you do, and the four of us will have to get together here in Rock Springs so I can reciprocate the ranch tour."

"I'd like that."

"That better not be who I think it is," Sarah says in the background.

"No, baby. It's not who you think it is," Mac replies.

"I'll let you go so you don't get into trouble. I hope to see you soon," I tell him with a smile.

"Talk to you later, man."

My plan originally was to go to Rock Springs and beg for Sky's forgiveness, but if she's going to be here in Walker Lake, I need a new plan. Also, if she's heading to talk to her parents, is it a good or bad thing? I have to hope it's a good thing.

My next move is to call Ben.

"Hey, man. Everything okay?" he answers.

Of course, he's going to think something's wrong. I never call him just because. I need to do better on that.

"Yeah, but I'm wondering if I can get your help with something."

"Anything," he says.

I explain the situation with Sky, what had happened way back then, what's going on now, and how she's on her way to talk to her parents as we speak.

"Wow. When you screw up, you really screw up, don't you?" Ben says, and he has a point.

"That's not helping," I grumble.

"Not trying to help, just speaking the truth." I can hear the smile in his voice.

"Listen, I have a farfetched plan, but I'm going to need your help because I don't think she's going to want to see or talk to me right now."

"Okay, hit me with it."

I go over the plan I came up with minutes ago, and Ben throws in a few suggestions. We work out the details, and I feel pretty confident by the time we end our call.

I'm already feeling better. It doesn't escape me; all the people Sky has brought into my life since she's been back.

When I returned to town, no one wanted to talk to me. Ben did, but even he kept his distance.

Thanks to Sky, I have people I can count on and call to ask for help.

It's like she's brought me back into the real world, and I don't plan on letting her down.

Chapter 22

Sky

The entire drive here, I tried to rehearse what I wanted to say to my parents, but I still have no idea. There are so many ways they could react that it's impossible to have a clear path and conversation.

I understand that, but that doesn't mean I like it. I like having a plan. I like knowing what direction things are going in and being in control of the situation. I won't have any of that here.

So, when I pull into the driveway, my nerves ratchet up a gear. I know I can do this. I know I have to do this. Thanks to Sarah and Mac, I have a solid game plan to get me where I want to be, and I'm not going to let them down.

I walk up the front porch steps, and my feet feel like they're covered in lead. It takes less than a minute to reach the front door, but it feels like hours before I finally ring the doorbell.

This time, it's my dad who opens the door. He looks at me but doesn't say anything. He just opens the door wider for me to step in. My mom is in her chair in the living room as I enter with my dad behind me.

"Did you come back to apologize for how you treated us?" my mom asks.

"I came back to say what I should have said that night. How dare you do that to him! How dare you do that to us! What kind of parent knowingly inflicts that kind of pain on their child?"

"How dare you—"

I hold up a hand to stall her because I'm nowhere near done. I know I'm leading with my emotions, but that's what needs to happen. "I never got over the heartbreak of what he did to me. It changed the entire trajectory of my life. You think it was for the best, but it wasn't. I was miserable in Dallas. I was miserable going to school, and every time something good happened, I wanted to reach out to my best friend, but I couldn't because you pushed him out of my life.

All the years we lost. You robbed us of that time and caused us unnecessary hurt. If you're not going to support my decisions, you don't deserve to be in my life. You don't get to control and manipulate me anymore."

With that, I pull the emergency credit card they gave me out of my pocket and put it on the table. I turn and walk out, ignoring anything they try to say to me.

I get in my car, and even though I'm only going next door to stay at Mac's family's lake house, I take the long way around the lake before pulling into the driveway.

I always loved it when Mac's family came to visit. Since Sarah made friends with him, we pretty much lived at this house with them. His sisters, Megan and Sage, craved more females because they were so sick of being with all their brothers, and the four of us got into so much trouble.

Even now, those memories make me smile. And when Corey came into the picture, he supported me in having friends.

He spent hours teasing me about what would happen when we got together. Was it pillow fights and doing our hair and makeup? I giggled and let him feed into whatever little fantasy he wanted.

Because, in reality, we spent a lot of time talking about him and the other guys. We took over the basement, watched movies, and ate all the junk food.

Life was so much easier and carefree back then.

I'm so lost in my memories that I nearly jump out of my skin when my phone rings. I'm standing in the living room in an empty house, staring off at the lake, when reality comes crashing down on me.

Why is Ben calling me?

"Hello?" I answer hesitantly.

"Hey, so don't be mad."

"For the record, Ben, anytime you open a conversation with 'hey, don't be mad,' a girl is instantly going to be mad. This might be why you're still single."

Ben laughs. "For the record, I'm single because I'm way too picky for the girls in this town. But now that you mention it, that might be why every time I've tried to talk to my sister lately, she gets pissed off because a lot of our conversations start that way."

"Yeah, I'd say there's a good chance that's it. What do you want, Ben?"

"So, I heard what was going on with you and Dash."

"Wait. How the hell did you hear that?" I ask, already irritated.

"I had to talk to him about something else, and I could tell something was going on, so I pulled it out of him. Hence the, don't be a mad part."

"Okay," I say, wanting to see where he's going with this conversation.

"I wanted to see how you're doing and ask if you want to grab lunch tomorrow. My treat."

"Ben, I don't want to be in town and bombarded with a million questions right now."

"I figured you'd say that, so I was thinking we'd grab lunch, and I'll bring you back here and show you my ranch." I can hear the smile in his voice.

"Wait, what ranch?" I ask, racking my brain and thinking he's told me something I've completely forgotten.

"Well, it's nothing big, but I bought myself a little piece of land. I've been working on it, and I just hired my first two ranch hands and want to show it off a little."

"I'd like that."

"Where are you staying? I'll pick you up tomorrow," he says.

"I'm staying at Sarah's husband's family place next door to my parents," I tell him.

"I know where that is. I'll see you tomorrow."

Once I get off the phone, I find the room that Sarah said I could use. It's her and Mac's when they're here.

After the long drive and the fight with my parents, the bed looks so comfortable. I figure I can lie down for a moment and rest before I get up and find something for dinner.

· · · • • · • • · ·

I wake up to someone at the door. I'm shocked when a quick look at my phone tells me it's eight in the morning. I still have my shoes on from yesterday.

I grab the sweatshirt from my bag on the chair, pull it over my head, and run my fingers through my hair as I answer the door.

I'm stunned to find my parents on the doorstep. "What are you doing here?"

"We saw the car in the driveway," my mom says, her voice emotionless.

I almost roll my eyes. "I suppose it'd be hard to miss being right next door."

"We came to apologize," my dad says.

"It's not my house, so I can't invite you in, but we can sit on the porch," I tell them. I want an easy out if things go badly, and it's harder to kick someone out of a house than to walk inside.

Once we've settled on the porch, my mother turns to me. "Being a parent isn't easy, no matter how much help you have. One day, you'll understand that. That being said, we made the best decision we could with the information we had. We didn't want you to change your whole life for some high school crush that wouldn't last beyond the first year of college. We didn't think you and Corey would ever amount to anything more.

"I know it's too little too late, but we would do things differently if we had another chance. So, we wanted to say that we're sorry for the decisions we made and how they affected you," my mother says.

It's the first time in my life I can remember her being genuine and vulnerable. My parents and I have never been close, but this feels like a big moment for us.

"Thank you. I don't know where things are going, but I need to know that you won't stand in my way again," I say, still a little defensive.

"We'll be completely out of the way," my mom says, holding her hands up in surrender.

With that, we hug before they return to their house. That's probably the most emotional moment I've ever had with them, and hopefully, it means we're on a good track.

I head inside and get ready for lunch with Ben. I've known him for years, and something tells me this isn't just lunch.

Chapter 23

DASH

I wait in Ben's barn, looking around nervously because I have no idea if this is going to work.

"She's going to love it; I promise," Jenna says. She's been here for hours helping with this, along with Natalie, Austin's sister.

I fucked up badly and figured it was going to take an amazingly grand gesture to win Sky back. Ben took my idea and ran with it. When he called in Jenna and Natalie, it ramped up to an even bigger scale. Ben also called Candy, the town librarian who recently had her own happily ever after right before Christmas.

The one thing I've always loved about small towns that I've missed is how people stick together. Candy doesn't know me, but she was here in a heartbeat because Ben asked for a favor. It reminds me of my time in the military. Someone always had your back.

With their help, we got Ben's barn set up before he left to pick up Sky. This is much bigger than anything I had in mind. But that doesn't mean it will work. Sky could take one look at me and leave. She could come in and yell and scream at me and still say no. She could hear me out, say no, and be out of town before dinner.

"Okay, we're going to get out of the way. I promise she's going to love it," Jenna says again, and she and Candy head out, leaving me alone in Ben's barn.

I calm myself until I hear tires on the gravel approaching the barn. Ben parks just out of view, but I can hear everything.

"What are we doing down here by the barn? I thought we were having lunch?" Sky asks.

"I only feel a little bad about deceiving you," Ben says as they round the corner.

Sky looks into the barn and freezes in the doorway, a look of pure awe on her face as she takes in the hundreds of twinkling lights filling the space. Chairs and a table made of hay with our lunch on it are surrounded by a heart made of hay. Rose petals and little battery-operated tea light candles are scattered everywhere.

The girls closed every window, so the only light coming into the barn is from the doorway where Sky is standing, which gives an amazing glow to the lights.

Ben suggested using his barn because he doesn't have any animals in it yet, and it makes the perfect setting. I owe him big time, whether or not this goes my way.

Ben nods at me from behind Sky before disappearing around the corner and leaving us alone.

"What is all this?" The awe in Sky's voice makes it all worth it.

"This is me saying I'm sorry. I didn't fight for us all those years ago, but I'm fighting for us now. Spending time with you made me realize my feelings for you back then were as real as my feelings for you now. When I walked away, all I did was cost us time.

"But you saw me when I wouldn't let anyone see me, and it made me realize that I'm still head over heels in love with you. I promise to make it up to you every day for the rest of our lives if you let me."

I take a deep breath, and right there in the middle of a heart made of hay and rose petals, I fall onto one knee and pull the ring out of my pocket—a ring that is a much grander version of the one I planned to buy for her years ago.

"You are the love of my life and the only woman I will ever love. Will you do me the incredible honor of being my wife?"

Then I wait.

Sky hasn't moved or made a sound since I started talking. The light shifts as she takes a hesitant step toward me, and I see the tears pouring down her face.

"Yes!" she says as she launches herself at me.

I barely have time to stand before she's in my arms. I slide the ring on her finger and pull her in for a kiss as our friends' cheers go up around us, along with the very distinct neigh of a horse as he stomps his feet.

"Jenna and Candy helped put this all together," I tell her.

"We also got pictures and video of it all for you. Congratulations!" Jenna says.

"And, of course, Ben was in on all of it," Sky says, laughing.

Even Phantom is here with all of us, and it seems perfect.

"You going to be happy staying here in town with me?" I ask her, just to be sure.

"It's all I've ever wanted. Everything else was just a filler for what I couldn't have." She smiles at me.

Ben pops a bottle of champagne. "Let's get this party started."

This is just the beginning.

Epilogue

Josh

The whole town is buzzing with news of Dash and Sky's engagement, and since Jenna was a huge part of it, she's been gushing about it nonstop. She's so excited for her friend.

Sitting across the table from her and watching her light up is one of the simple joys. This girl has held my attention for years, but I've had to get my fill from a distance.

After all, it's harder when the girl of your dreams happens to be your best friend's daughter. I have to seem interested enough to make my best friend happy but not so interested it causes suspicion.

It wasn't always like this. Jenna and I were friends. She called me Uncle Josh for a long time, but when her parents moved here to Walker Lake, I couldn't follow.

My marriage was falling apart at that time, so I stuck around long enough to file for divorce and sort everything out. Then I followed them out here.

By then, Jenna was almost twenty, and seeing her for the first time in years was like a punch in the gut. But I'd never do anything to destroy my friendship with her dad, so here I sit across the table from her, soaking in what's going to have to get me through the next month.

"Decorating that barn was so much fun, but watching it unfold was like something right out of a romance novel; it was so romantic and beautiful. If I ever get married, I hope my proposal is half as perfect," she gushes with a dreamy smile.

The thought of her marrying someone else doesn't sit well with me. I want her to be happy, but trusting her with another guy might be more than I can handle.

"You're going to come, right, Josh?" Jenna asks.

She stopped calling me Uncle Josh about the time I moved to Walker Lake.

"Sorry, my mind was elsewhere. Coming where?" I ask, having been caught with my mind wandering.

"To the Fourth of July festival with us." She giggles.

"Of course he is. I'm not letting him sit at home and not do anything for the Fourth of July," her dad says.

How do you tell your best friend that you can't go to the July Fourth festival because you're in love with his daughter and have been for way too long?

We keep getting thrown together no matter how hard I try to keep my distance. Some of it is Jenna's doing, but a lot of it is her father's doing. Her dad's been helping her brothers a lot lately, looking at different ranches they've been looking to buy. Her mom does a lot of volunteer work, so when Jenna needs something, her dad asks me.

But I'm only so strong, and I'm starting to wonder if moving to Walker Lake was the right thing to do.

When Jenna looks at me and smiles, our gazes lock for a moment, and my heart races. There's a thrill in having her eyes on me. It's a high that no drug could ever give me. I know I'm going to be a glutton for punishment.

"I wouldn't miss it for the world," I tell them honestly.

· · · ● · ● · · ·

Want more from Dash and Sky? **Get the bonus epilogue when you sign up for my newsletter!**

Get Josh and Jenn'as story in **The Cowboy and his Best Friend's Daughter.**

Want Mac and Sarah's? Grab it in **The Cowboy and His Secret.**

More Books by Kaci M. Rose

Walker Lake, Texas

The Cowboy and His Beauty - Dash and Sky

The Cowboy and His Best Friend's Daughter – Josh and Jenna

Other Books Walker Lake Books

Taken By The Cowboy – North and Candy

The Cowboy and His City Girl – Chase and Mandy

Rock Springs Texas Series

The Cowboy and His Runaway – Blaze and Riley

The Cowboy and His Best Friend – Sage and Colt

The Cowboy and His Obsession – Megan and Hunter

The Cowboy and His Sweetheart – Jason and Ella

The Cowboy and His Secret – Mac and Sarah

Rock Springs Weddings Novella

Rock Springs Box Set 1-5 + Bonus Content

Cowboys of Rock Springs

The Cowboy and His Mistletoe Kiss – Lilly and Mike

The Cowboy and His Valentine – Maggie and Nick

The Cowboy and His Vegas Wedding – Royce and Anna

The Cowboy and His Angel – Abby and Greg

The Cowboy and His Christmas Rockstar – Savannah and Ford

The Cowboy and His Billionaire – Brice and Kayla

The Cowboy and His Sleeping Beauty – Miles and Rose

Connect with Kaci M. Rose

Kaci M. Rose writes steamy small town cowboys. She also writes under Kaci Rose and there she writes wounded military heroes, giant mountain men, sexy rock stars, and even more there. Connect with her below!

Website

Facebook

Kaci Rose Reader's Facebook Group

Goodreads

Book Bub

Join Kaci M. Rose's VIP List (Newsletter)

About Kaci M Rose

Kaci M Rose writes cowboy, hot and steamy cowboys set in all town anywhere you can find a cowboy.

She enjoys horseback riding and attending a rodeo where is always looking for inspiration.

Kaci grew on a small farm/ranch in Florida where they raised cattle and an orange grove. She learned to ride a four-wheeler instead of a bike (and to this day still can't ride a bike) and was driving a tractor before she could drive a car.

Kaci prefers the country to the city to this day and is working to buy her own slice of land in the next year or two!

Kaci M Rose is the Cowboy Romance alter ego of Author Kaci Rose.

See all of Kaci Rose's Books here.

Please Leave a Review!

I love to hear from my readers! Please **head over to your favorite store and leave a review** of what you thought of this book!

Made in the USA
Columbia, SC
23 September 2024